*For my mum.*

# chapter one

Edge of Flight. That's the climb that always defeats me. Seventy feet of hard sandstone up a perfect arête.

Tomorrow I'll be standing at the base of it, my harness weighed down with gear. I'm already running through the moves in my head. I'm already imagining Edge of Flight.

*I raise my right foot to a tiny ledge just two inches off the ground, then reach for the first handhold—a hump of rock that fits in my right palm like a softball.*

1

"Ready to climb," I say over my shoulder to Rusty.

"On belay," Rusty says. He tightens the rope in the belay device clipped to his harness.

I grip the arête with my left hand, then lean my weight to the right. I raise my left foot and place it on a tiny nub of rock so that I'm standing on my tiptoes on two square inches of stone. My fingers keep me balanced against the cliff face.

"Climbing," I say.

"Climb on," says Rusty.

It's all balance for the next forty feet up. Like most female climbers, balance is what I'm good at. The guys can crank the overhangs, but for me, climbing is a high-wire act. I'm defying gravity on a vertical plane. I'm moving on an updraft of muscle tone and thin air.

On the ascent, I find the tiny chinks and cracks in the rock to lay my pro, otherwise known as protective gear. I clip the rope to my pro in case I fall. But I know I can make *the first forty feet without falling. I've done it before.*

*Then I come to the crux.*

*That's where the microholds run out and there's nothing more to grab or stand on. Nothing to grip, to keep me moving up the flat, smooth rock face.*

*I perch on the ball of my right foot. There is no foothold for my left. So I hold it crossed behind my right for balance. My arms stretch wide on either side of the arête, gripping tiny nubs of rock. My cheek presses against the stone. I tilt my head to look up at a big pistol-hold grip far above. I know from watching Rusty climb that once I get to the pistol-hold grip, I'm home free. After that, it's all chunky handholds and footholds to the top. But how can I make it across the gap?*

*It's all technique, says Rusty.*

*Easy for him to say. He's six-foot-two and has arms like a monkey. I'm five-five and still working on my technique. But I've figured out a way to pull this climb.*

*I must let go with my right hand so that I'm touching the rock at only two points of contact—right foot, left hand. Then, I have to circle my right hand upward, while rising onto tiptoe with my right foot, like a dancer on pointe. But while I move—and this is the critical thing—I must hold my body perfectly balanced, like a ball poised on a juggler's fingertip. And when my outstretched hand reaches the very top of its arc, I must grab the pistol-hold grip and pull up. Pull up as hard as I can.*

*I know that's what I have to do. But every time I get to the crux, I lose my nerve. I'm standing forty feet above the ground, and my last piece of pro—a tiny metal nut wedged into a crack, with the rope clipped to it by a carabiner—is stuck in the rock five feet below me. If I lose my balance and come off the rock, I'll fall ten feet before the rope jerks me to a stop. But if the weight of my body rips the nut out of the crack, I'll go into an uncontrolled twenty-foot fall. A fall that will bring me dangerously close to hitting the ground.*

*So although I know I need to let go with my right hand, I can't do it. Instead, I always hesitate, chicken out, let myself slither downward in a controlled fall and bunny-hop into the safety of Rusty's belay. Then I shout for Rusty to lower me down.*

*But not this time, I tell myself.*

*This time, I will work up the nerve to pull Edge of Flight.*

## chapter two

"What can I git y'all?"

I look up to see the waitress standing beside our table. She's in her forties with dolled-up blond hair and thick black mascara. I haven't even looked at the menu. So I take a quick glance while Jeb and Rusty order chicken and grits.

"Could I get the soup of the day?" I say. "And the pecan pie, please."

I try to pronounce it like they do down here—"p'kaahn," not "pee-can." But the moment I open my mouth, everyone in the diner knows I'm not from the South. The men at the other tables glance at us. They're not hostile, just fitting us into place in their minds. *Two high school boys from Fayetteville and their Yankee girlfriend.*

"Y'all goin' campin'?" the waitress asks.

"Climbin'," says Jeb. "Up at Sam's Throne."

"Better be careful. It's huntin' season," says the waitress. "Some a them good ol' boys'll shoot at anything that moves."

She turns away from our table and crosses back to the lunch counter, flirting and joking with some of the good ol' boys. Then she disappears through the swinging door into the kitchen to place our order. This diner is the only place to eat in Mount Judea, two hours from Fayetteville and the last town on the map before driving into the woods of Arkansas' Ozark Mountains.

Judea—as in the land of the ancient Jewish tribes in the Bible. Only the locals here pronounce it Judy—as in Judge Judy, woman of snap decisions and strong-set opinions. There's no room here for weakness and doubt.

The waitress brings our order as a pickup truck pulls into the gravel parking space in front of the diner. The word spreads quickly that the hunter has bagged his game. Everyone goes outside to have a look at the dead bobcat lolling in the flatbed. I don't really want to stand there gawking at a dead bobcat. It's kind of creepy. But I don't want to be left alone in the diner either. So I follow Jeb and Rusty outside.

The men are all gathered around the pickup. The bobcat looks like a limp mound of black-and-tawny fur. Its head hangs off the end of the flatbed, and its tongue sticks out from between white, jagged teeth. I turn away, feeling sick.

In the opposite corner of the parking lot, a sheriff's deputy is talking to two bikers. They are big, beefy guys, who straddle their motorbikes and wear heavy boots, planted in the dirt. They lean forward aggressively on their handlebars. One has a leather jacket with a patch of the Grim Reaper on the back. The other has a muscle shirt on, with tattoos on his shoulders and down his arms.

They both have black beards and long black hair in ponytails.

The cop finishes talking to them and strolls over to the men gathered around the dead bobcat in the pickup.

"Make sure you check his hunting license, deputy!" one of the bikers calls after him, jeering.

The deputy—a tall, lanky man—looks embarrassed. But he says, "Mind if I check your license, Bill?"

"Not a problem, Jim," says the hunter.

The hunter opens the truck's passenger-side door and reaches inside. When he comes back out, he's holding some paperwork in one hand and a rifle in the other. He gives the bikers a don't-mess-with-me look.

The deputy glances at the paperwork. "That's just fine, Bill. Thanks."

"Not a problem," says Bill. He stows the paperwork back in the truck. But not the rifle.

"I expect folks around here to follow the law," the deputy declares, speaking to everyone and no one.

The biker in the Grim Reaper jacket laughs. "We'll sure enough follow you, deputy," he says. "Y'all just lead, and we'll follow right along."

The two bikers kick their motorcycles into gear and roar off. The wheels spray gravel on the men standing beside the truck. The hunter, Bill, raises his rifle in the air, like he's about to fire a warning shot. The deputy puts his hand on the muzzle. "That'll be enough," he says.

I turn to Rusty. "Maybe we shouldn't climb this weekend." My fingers itch for Edge of Flight. But I'm getting a bad feeling about camping out in the local woods.

"We're climbin'," Rusty says. He swings open the screen door and trots back inside the diner.

It's really only half a diner. The other half of the old wooden building is set up like a general store. It sells fishing tackle, guns, motor oil, canned food, chocolate bars, cigarettes and chewing tobacco. Rusty picks three neon-orange hunting caps up off a dusty shelf.

"I ain't wearin' one a them things," says Jeb. "Y'all want me to look like a fool?"

"Better a live fool than a dead fool," says Rusty. He sets one of the caps on his head and grins.

"Maybe it's better if we go back home," I say. "My mom could use some help packing."

"No way, Vanisha," says Rusty. "This is your last chance to pull Edge of Flight before you leave."

## chapter three

The sun is setting by the time we finish eating and pile back into Jeb's truck. The sky gets darker as we leave town, cross the bridge over the river and drive up the dirt road into the forest. The road is narrow, bumpy and steep. Now and then we have to pull over, leaning halfway into the ditch, to make room for the headlights of another vehicle coming toward us. Finally, the truck grinds up a set of switchbacks and reaches the top of the ridge. Jeb parks on the side of the road.

It's not a campsite, really. It's a patch of hard-packed dirt, with a few rocks and weeds sticking out. In the center of the patch, three logs surround a ring of stones. Inside the ring, a pile of charred embers marks a sign of campfires past. The moon, nearly full, floats above a mass of thick gray clouds. Mosquitoes throng around us.

Rusty gets a campfire going by the light of his headlamp. He spears three marshmallows on a stick and roasts them. "Sugar." He pops the gooey mess into his mouth. "My drug of choice."

"You're gonna need treatment, boy," Jeb says. "Rehab. Sucralose injections."

Rusty grins. "I'm not an addict." He spears more marshmallows on his stick. "I've got it under control."

I fish a marshmallow out of the bag and set it to roast over the fire. I hold it steady in that sweet spot where it will turn crispy-golden without catching on fire.

Jeb plunks himself down next to me. "You're mighty quiet." I scooch over to give him some room. Jeb's a football player—the kind of guy whose shoulders take up two seats on a Greyhound bus. "Thinkin' about movin'?" he says.

"Yeah, that and college," I say.

"You don't sound too keen."

"No. I guess I'm not." When I applied, it seemed to make sense to go back to the University of Vermont. That's where most of my high school friends are going. After all, I have only been in Arkansas for a year. I followed my mom on a visiting professorship position at the University of Fayetteville.

Vermont's home, kind of. Mom's a poetry professor. So we moved around a lot while I was growing up. Turns out there aren't a lot of full-time jobs for people whose only skill is picking apart metaphors. So Mom moved from one little New England college to another, always hunting for a better position. I was happy when she got a tenure-track position at the University of Vermont four years ago, and I thought we would finally stay in one place. But last year, my senior year of high school, she decided to take the Fayetteville job. So we moved to Arkansas, of all places.

If I hadn't met Rusty and Jeb, if they hadn't taught me to rock climb, my life this year would have been a total write-off. But I did meet them. And they introduced me to a different way of living. I was just starting to get the hang of climbing. I was just starting to enjoy being out here. And now, I have to move again. I'm not so sure I want to go back.

"What is it you're fixin' to study?" says Jeb.

"General arts," I say, without enthusiasm. "History. English lit. Philosophy."

"Sounds practical," Jeb says sarcastically. He's only ribbing me, but this comment touches a nerve.

I reel in my marshmallow. It is caramel on the outside and nearly liquid in the center. Perfect.

"Okay, smarty," I say through a mouthful of marshmallow. "What's your plan?"

Jeb shrugs. "Get a job. Pay off my truck. Move out. Get my own place."

"What about long-term?"

"Save up for a high-def TV," he answers. "Watch lots of sports."

I slap him on his granite-hard shoulder. "You're pathetic."

"You should take outdoor ed, Vanisha," Rusty says from his log on the other side of the campfire. "You'd be good at it."

The truth is, Rusty's the only one of us who knows what he's doing with his life. He's already started studying to be an ambulance attendant. He jumped right into the summer semester after high school finished in June. He'll be great at it too. Rusty never panics in an emergency. He never seems to have a moment of doubt about anything he's doing. Unlike me.

"I can't take outdoor ed. My mom would never pay for it," I say. "She doesn't think it's a 'real' university degree."

"Whattya mean 'real'?" says Jeb.

"You know, like history or philosophy. Or science," I say. I wish I was good at science.

Then at least I could be something practical, like a doctor or a veterinarian. "She thinks you're not well-educated unless you have a real university degree."

"Well, 'scuse my dumb ass for livin'," drawls Jeb, laying on a hillbilly accent.

"I didn't say I agreed with it."

"But you're going along with it," says Rusty. "Come on, Vanisha. What do you really want to do with your life?"

I shrug. But the truth is, lately, I've had a crazy idea in my head. I want to do something different. Something adventurous. Something meaningful. I picture myself rappelling out of helicopters and saving people from drowning. I imagine combing the woods for lost children. Or digging out skiers buried alive in avalanches.

But what do I know about that stuff? I was never even interested in the outdoors before I met Jeb and Rusty. And what if I'm no good at it? What if people die on my watch?

Doesn't it make more sense to go to university, like I'm supposed to? Go get my BA and a job in an office somewhere, or in government? Or become a professor like my mother, writing essays about dead poets and publishing them in journals nobody reads?

My mom would admire me if I became a professor. She'd look down on me if I didn't get a real university degree. Besides, I've already been accepted to the University of Vermont. Mom's paid the tuition deposit. School starts in two weeks.

So I hesitate at this crux of my life. I'm afraid to make the move I know I should. Just like I hesitate at the crux of Edge of Flight.

Jeb yawns and goes to pull his mat and sleeping bag out of the truck. He and Rusty bed down on the ground beside the campfire.

But I just sit on the log, stare into the fire and wonder why I can't make a decision that would put my life on a different course.

Jeb wriggles into his sleeping bag. He lays his head at my feet, like a loyal Saint Bernard. He looks up at me. "You can sleep in the back of the truck, if you're a-skeered of the critters," he says.

"I'm not a-skeered of the critters," I say. I glance up at the dark clouds. "I just don't want to get rained on."

I take my sleeping bag and mat from the truck and lie down on the ground next to the guys. I ignore the rustlings in the underbrush, the mosquitoes droning in my ears, the faint sounds of hunters' voices drifting through the dark woods and the thought of bikers with tattoos and leather jackets.

I close my eyes and try to sleep.

I am practicing not wimping out.

## chapter four

The next morning, Jeb cooks up a mess of bacon and eggs over the campfire. After breakfast, we pack our gear for a day of climbing. A light drizzle is falling, not much more than a mist. Still, we should get moving before the cliffs are soaked and slippery. But Rusty's a total gear-head. He can't resist showing us the new piece of pro he just bought with his part-time job at the climbing gym.

"Check this out," says Rusty.

With a metallic clinking, Rusty pulls a massive rack of pro from his backpack. There are dozens of nuts and hexes of all different sizes. But one brand-new piece of equipment stands out. It's a huge camming device—a spring-loaded gizmo with sharp-toothed metal gears at one end and a trigger at the other. The gears on the cam are the size of Jeb's fist, which is as big as a trucker's long-haul coffee mug.

Rusty pulls the trigger, and the gears retract. "You stick it into the crack," he says. Then he releases the trigger and the gears spring out. "And it grabs ahold."

"Sweet..." Jeb drools. He reaches out to hold it, like it's a precious gemstone. "We gotta pull Chuck's Crack with this baby."

"Dude, yeah."

They sit in silence for a few seconds, soaking up the awesomeness of the cam. Then Rusty says, "Let's climb."

He reloads the pro into his backpack and sticks his orange hunting cap on his head. I'm already wearing mine. Jeb shoves his into his back pocket. A corner of it sticks out like a flag waving on his butt.

"Good way to protect your brain," says Rusty sarcastically.

"Listen, boy," says Jeb. "I'd rather have brain damage than get my weenie shot off."

We're camping at the top of the escarpment, but we have to get to the bottom to climb it. We set slings around a couple of trees, clip two carabiners to the slings and loop the rope through the 'biners. Now we've got a top rope to rappel down.

On the way down, I hear the gunfire from hunters hidden somewhere amid the woods below. It's cool being this high up, dangling from a rope like a kid on a swing. There's a feeling of freedom—one of the things I like best about climbing. But soon I'm among the trees again, my feet touching the dirt and rocks at the bottom of the cliff.

Once everyone's down, we pull in the rope and walk about a hundred feet to the base of Edge of Flight. When I look up, the cliff face glistens with rain drops. I try out the first handhold. My fingers slip off right away. For a balancy route like this one, it's already too wet to climb.

"Sorry, Vanisha," says Rusty.

"It's okay," I say. "Maybe tomorrow."

I'm disappointed because I've been psyching myself up for this. But deep inside, I also feel a tiny bit relieved.

Maybe I couldn't have pulled the crux. Maybe I would have stalled or fallen. Now, I don't have to test myself. And it's not even my fault for wimping out. It's the weather. No one can control the weather.

I hate my cowardly thoughts, but I can't stop them. Why do I have to be so afraid?

"What do we do now?" asks Rusty.

"Chuck's Crack!" Jeb bellows and probably scares off half the animals in the woods. The hunters are going to love him for that.

Rusty grins. "All right. You leading?"

"You bet," says Jeb. He's obviously dying to test Rusty's new cam.

We walk about fifty feet along the cliff to the base of Chuck's Crack. Rusty sets his backpack on the ground. He and Jeb start roping in.

The name Chuck's Crack pretty much describes the climb. It's a crack, about five inches wide, that runs upward in a straight, vertical line from the base of the cliff.

Three-quarters of the way up, the crack ends at a rock shelf that sticks out and forms an overhang. The overhang keeps Chuck's Crack dry in drizzly weather like today's. But getting over the rock shelf is the crux of the climb.

Jeb picks up Rusty's new cam, along with some big hexes and wedges. He clips them onto his climbing harness. Then he makes a fist with one of his enormous hands, sticks it into the crack, turns his fist horizontally and pulls back on it. His hand is locked into the crack like a deadbolt. He does the same thing with his other fist, fitting it into the crack above the first one.

"Ready to climb," he says.

"On belay," says Rusty.

Jeb locks his elbows, leans back on his straight arms and jumps off the ground. He plants both feet flat against the rock face, one on either side of the crack. "Climbing," he says.

"Climb on," says Rusty.

Jeb's climb is a show of pure physical strength. His technique is simple. He takes one fist, shoves it into the crack. Takes the other fist, shoves it into the crack above the first one. Then he leans back on his arms and jumps his feet up the rock face. Fist-fist-jump. Fist-fist-jump. Repeat all the way up. His legs aren't doing much more than keeping him braced against the rock. His arms are doing all the work, pulling all the weight. And Jeb must weigh at least 250 pounds.

"How does he do that?" I ask Rusty.

"Jeb bench-presses three hundred," he says.

"Right," I say. "I guess I'll just stick to the balancy stuff."

"Good plan," says Rusty.

Jeb keeps going until he reaches the spot below the overhang. "Hey, y'all! Watch this!" he shouts.

He unclips Rusty's new cam from his harness, kisses it, jams it into the crack and clips the rope to it with a carabiner. Rusty keeps a tight hold on the belay. Now comes the crux. Jeb keeps one fist stuck in the crack, reaches over his head and grabs the lip of the overhang with his other hand. "Gimme some slack!" he yells.

Rusty lets out a bit of rope. Jeb takes his other fist out of the crack and circles it around to grab the lip of the overhang. His legs swing out. Now he's hanging from the rock shelf, his feet dangling in midair.

"I got ya, buddy!" Rusty yells.

Jeb curls his arms at the elbows, like he's doing a chin-up. His head comes up to the edge of the overhang. He reaches an arm out and grabs the trunk of a skinny tree growing on top of the rock ledge. Rusty lets out some more slack. Jeb hoists a knee over the ledge and scrambles to the top.

He stands up, hanging on to the tree for safety, and looks down at us.

"CHUUUUCK'S CRAAAACK!" he hollers, pumping his fist in the air.

"Dude! The tree's off-route!" Rusty shouts, like he has to find something to give Jeb a hard time about.

"No it ain't!" Jeb shouts back.

From the overhang, it's only a few more feet to the top of the cliff. But instead of topping out the climb, Jeb edges back to the lip of the overhang. He peers down, then turns to face away from us, like a diver about to attempt a backflip.

"You got me, buddy?" he shouts.

Rusty ratchets the rope in tight. "Got ya!"

"What's he—?" I say. But before I can finish my sentence, Jeb lets out a holler and jumps off the overhang.

"WEEEEE-HAAAAAH!"

From the ledge forty feet above the ground, Jeb flies through the air. He falls down...down...When he reaches the end of the rope, it catches him with a jerk. The force yanks Rusty forward, nearly pulling him off the ground. Jeb swings on the end of the rope toward the rock face. He braces his hands and feet to cushion the impact. He makes contact. Springs back. Swings toward the rock face again. Makes contact again, more softly this time. He ends up dangling from the rope five feet below the overhang, laughing like an idiot.

"What did you do that for, dude?" Rusty shouts.

"Wanted to test out your new cam!" Jeb shouts back. "It's bombproof, man!"

"Thanks a lot!" Rusty yells back. I can tell he's not happy about the unnecessary wear and tear on his new gear.

"He's crazy," I say. Rusty just shakes his head and continues belaying while Jeb pulls the overhang again and tops out the climb.

It takes Jeb a few minutes to set up a belay from the top of the cliff. Then he hauls in the rope. The end of it dangles between Rusty and me.

"Your turn?" Rusty asks, holding out the rope end.

"Are you kidding?" I say. I stick my fist into the crack and turn it sideways. The edges of my hand don't even graze the rock.

"That's not the only way to pull this climb," Rusty grins. He ties the rope into his harness. "Ready to climb!" he shouts up to Jeb.

"On belay!" Jeb shouts back.

Rusty winks at me. "Climbing!"

"Climb on!" says Jeb.

## chapter five

If Jeb is the Incredible Hulk of the climbing world, Rusty is Spider-Man. If Jeb is all muscle, Rusty is all technique. Instead of sticking his fist into the crack like Jeb, Rusty wraps his fingers around one edge of it. Then he leans sideways, so the right side of his body—arm, shoulder, ribcage, leg—is pressed against the rock face to the right of the crack. Staying sideways, he probes the cliff face with his toes for footholds. He finds a chunk of rock to brace his feet against, pushes up, crosses one hand over the other to reach higher into the crack, and slides his body sideways up the wall.

"Cool," I say.

"Classic layback." Rusty grins.

Classic layback. Rusty makes it sound easy. He makes it look easy too. Effortless. But I've climbed enough to realize how much skill it takes to find the perfect tension between arms and legs—to maintain that point of balance that keeps Rusty pressed against the wall, not swinging out like a barn door on a loose hinge.

Moving smoothly, Rusty stops only to remove the pro Jeb laid on the way up and clip it on to his harness. Sometimes his footholds are nubs of rock. Sometimes he jams his foot into the crack. But always, he stays with his right flank pressed against the rock face, shimmying up it sideways.

When he reaches the overhang, Rusty stays sideways. He finds a handhold on the underside of the ledge with his right hand, reaches out and grabs the lip with his left. But instead of letting go and dangling like Jeb,

Rusty crosses his right leg and jams his right foot into some kind of a foothold on the underside of the ledge. Now he's pressed against the underside of the ledge like a fly on a ceiling. Somehow—I have no idea how—he swings his left leg up and hooks his left foot over the ledge. He takes an overhand swipe with his right arm—like a basketball player doing a J-hook—and manages to grab the trunk of the scrawny tree on top of the ledge. He swings the rest of his body over the ledge just as Jeb yells, "I told ya the tree was on-route!"

"You were right!" Rusty yells back. He stands up, jumps onto the chunky handholds, and in a few minutes, he's topped out the climb.

"Good climb!" I shout.

Rusty's face peeks over the top of the cliff. "Come on, try it!" he shouts back.

I run my fingers along the edge of the crack, testing out the hold. I'm tempted, even though I know it's beyond my skill level. But the rain begins to pour down harder. Soon, the cliff will be soaked and water will stream down the crack like a drainpipe.

"Not in the rain," I shout.

"Okay. We're coming down."

I know it'll take a few minutes for the guys to set up a top rope and rappel down. While I'm waiting, I realize I need to go to the bathroom. Of course, there's no outhouse in sight. This is the one situation in my life where I often wish I'd been born a guy.

I walk into the woods and look for a big tree, a bush or a hillock to give me some privacy in case the guys come back before I'm done. But the knee-high grass, coiling vines and slim, snaky trees aren't ideal. I push farther into the woods, checking that my orange cap is still on my head. I don't want to be mistaken for a stray deer or an undersized black bear.

I listen for gunshots but don't hear any. Maybe the hunters are in another part of the woods. Maybe they've taken shelter from the rain. A few steps farther on, the ground dips down. A steep slope leads to a hidden ravine. I hang on to the trunk of a skinny tree and lower myself down the slope. It's not the most comfortable place for a pee, but at least it's out of sight.

I've just finished answering the call of nature when I hear Jeb call, "Vanisha? Where are ya?"

"I'm over here," I call back. "It's okay. I'm just..."

I turn to get a better foothold on the steep slope and see something at the bottom that makes me freeze.

Jeb thrashes through the underbrush toward me. "Vanisha?" He reaches the top of the ravine and makes his way down to stand beside me. Then he stops too.

"Sweet Lord Jesus," Jeb whispers.

At the bottom of the ravine, someone has planted a field of marijuana.

## chapter six

"Let's get out of here," I say.

"Aw, come on," says Jeb. "Let's go take a look."

"Take a look at what?" says Rusty.

"That." Jeb points at the marijuana patch below.

"Don't be an idiot, Jeb," I say.

Before I can stop him, Jeb starts off down the slope toward the marijuana field, half running and half sliding in the rain-soaked mud.

"Don't be a party pooper, Vanisha," he says.

Rusty reaches out and grabs his arm. "Slow down."

"What for?" he asks.

"Just slow down." Rusty steps ahead of him and begins picking his way down the hill, pushing aside each twig and leaf. He looks like an animal tracker following a trail. Or maybe an army scout, looking for enemy booby traps.

He's almost reached the marijuana field when he stops so suddenly that Jeb nearly bumps into him.

"What the—?" says Jeb.

"Look," says Rusty. He points at the tangle of vines and tree branches in front of him.

I can't see anything except dripping-wet greenery. Jeb obviously can't either, because he takes another step forward.

Rusty sticks out an arm to block his way. "Look in front of you, dude."

I inch closer and see it—a thin metal wire stretched at chest-height through the bush.

Raindrops hang from the wire, bulging before dropping off.

"What is it?" says Jeb.

"Don't touch it," Rusty says. He walks along beside the wire. Jeb and I follow him. It leads to the trunk of a large tree—bigger than the other skinny, twisted trees in this ragged patch of woods. The tree is straight and solid, covered in smooth gray bark. At eye level, the trunk splits, forming a Y-shaped crook. I stare into the crook. Something ugly stares back at me. The barrel of a rifle. The rifle is rigged to go off if someone triggers the wire.

"That would've got you right in the head," Rusty says to Jeb.

Jeb gives a low whistle. "Thanks for lookin' out for me, brother." He thumps Rusty on the shoulder. Then he ducks under the trip wire and wades into the marijuana patch.

"Jeb! Are you crazy!" I hiss at him. I don't know why I'm whispering. There's no one else around, as far as I can tell. But there might be guard dogs, or even human guards, hiding in the bushes. A picture flashes across my mind of the two bikers outside the diner last night who were laughing at the deputy. Laughing.

Jeb plucks a sprig of marijuana and sticks it in his hair like a blossom. "If you go to San Francisco..." he starts singing in a loud, goofy voice. "Be sure to wear some floooo-wers in your hair!"

Rusty turns to me with a disgusted expression on his face. "Come on, Vanisha. If Jeb wants to act like an idiot, that's his problem. I'm getting out of here."

Rusty and I turn and start hiking out of the ravine. It's not like Rusty to leave anyone in a dangerous situation. But I'm thinking he's just messing with Jeb. He's probably figuring his buddy won't want to stay in an illegal plantation in the middle of the woods alone.

Sure enough, we haven't gone more than a couple of steps when Jeb catches up to us. "Aw, y'all are no fun."

"Marijuana is for losers, dude," says Rusty. "I came here to climb. Not fool around with drugs."

That makes Jeb shut his mouth. He may be a big goof, but he respects Rusty's climbing ability. Rusty doesn't need drugs to prove he's cool. He just pulls a flawless climb, like he did today on Chuck's Crack, and it's obvious. He's cool. No argument about it.

Jeb plucks the marijuana sprig out of his hair and tosses it into the undergrowth. He falls into line behind us and doesn't mention the marijuana again. Still, I feel edgy and unsettled as we tramp in silence back to the cliff. The rain beats on the hood of my windbreaker. My shoes squelch on the wet ground.

When we arrive at the cliff face, it is too wet to climb.

"Chimney?" I ask.

Rusty nods. "Chimney."

We walk a few minutes along the bluff line. Rusty stops and shrugs off his backpack. In front of us, the solid rock wall looks as though it's been cracked open like an egg. The crack, several feet wide, runs from the bottom of the cliff to the top. It is filled with tumbled-down boulders and huge rock slabs.

The Chimney.

## chapter seven

The entrance to the Chimney is hard to find if you don't know where to look. But Rusty has been here many times before. He drops to his hands and knees where a massive rock slab lies diagonally across the crack. Beneath it is a small, triangular gap. Rusty crawls through the gap, pushing his backpack ahead of him. I follow. Jeb brings up the rear.

Inside the Chimney, the ground is dry and sandy. There is enough room to stand.

The smell of damp stone fills the cool air. We're sheltered from the rain. I look up but can't see the sky. The Chimney is filled with boulders like a vertical obstacle course.

Rusty turns to me. "You first?"

"Sure." I jump atop the first boulder.

I'm not roped in, but it doesn't matter. Any kid who has ever scrambled up a rocky hill could climb the Chimney. The first boulder leads to another, then another, zigzagging upward like a crazy stone staircase built for giants.

About halfway up the Chimney, a massive rock ledge seems to completely block the route. But I remember in one corner, a sloping slab of rock leads to a hole through the ledge. I crawl up the slab, first on all fours, and finally squirming on my belly, as the slab angles closer and closer to the rock ledge. At last, I wriggle my head and shoulders through the hole, flip over and haul myself on top of the ledge.

Not much farther now to the top. I scramble up a boulder, which leads me to another, smaller, rock ledge. I can see where the Chimney ends and the tree branches of the forest begin. I feel the rain and smell the earthy dampness of wet leaves.

The Chimney is narrow here. The rock walls are so close together, I can stand in the middle and press one hand against each wall. But there are no more boulders to climb. The next part is pure chimneying.

I press my back flat against one wall and raise my legs so my knees are bent and my feet are jammed against the other wall. The rocks are wet, but my shoes have good traction, and I'm wedged in so tight, I can't fall. Straightening my legs, I scooch my back higher up the Chimney wall. Then I walk my legs up the opposite wall and scooch my back higher again, working my way to the top.

I climb out of the Chimney and onto my knees on the damp forest floor. When I turn to look down, Rusty is standing on the ledge below.

"You climb like my granny!" he calls up.

"Let's see you do it!" I shout down.

Rusty spreads his arms and presses his palms against the Chimney's walls. He springs up and plants his feet against the walls too. Then he clambers up, like a boy climbing a door frame. In only a couple of seconds, he's standing beside me.

"Sweet," I say.

Rusty shrugs. "It works." He peers down the Chimney. "Wonder where Jeb got to."

I look down. No sign of Jeb. "Maybe he's stuck in the hole in the big ledge," I say. "Too many marshmallows last night."

"Marshmallows aren't fattening if you eat 'em quick," says Rusty.

I shake my head. "You just go on believing that."

"Hey, Jeb! Ya moron!" Rusty shouts in the friendly insulting way guys can talk to each other.

From inside the cliff, we hear Jeb. "Down here!"

"You stuck?" Rusty shouts.

"Naw. C'mon back in here, y'all. I found somethin'."

"It better not be another drug plantation," I mutter.

Rusty shrugs and lowers himself into the Chimney. "Come on."

We climb down but reach the soft sandy ground at the bottom of the Chimney and still don't see Jeb.

"Where are you?" Rusty calls.

"Over here!" Jeb's voice sounds as if it's coming from the depths of the cliff. Like Jonah in the belly of the whale. Living in the South is turning my mind biblical.

Rusty pulls his headlamp out of his backpack. As an ambulance attendant in training, Rusty always travels fully equipped. He's even got a first-aid kit in his pack. It's fully stocked with gauze bandages, alcohol wipes, emergency snake-bite serum and all kinds of other stuff.

Rusty scans the Chimney with his headlamp until it lights up a tunnel that leads deeper into the cliff. "Jeb?"

"In here." His voice comes from the direction of the tunnel. So we drop to our knees and begin to crawl through it.

At first, Rusty's headlamp shows only the sandstone walls of the tunnel. They are carved into curvy shapes, as though a river flowed through here thousands of years ago. Then suddenly the beam widens and diffuses. We are in some kind of a cave.

"Jeb!" calls Rusty. His voice echoes in the emptiness.

He stands and reaches his hand down to help me. Rusty's grip is strong, and even after I'm on my feet, I don't feel like letting go. The cave is damp, cool and eerie. Apart from Rusty's headlamp, the only light comes from a small air shaft at the far end.

"Jeb?" Rusty calls.

A hand comes down on my shoulder. I jump.

"Boo!" Jeb shouts.

"You idiot!" I scream.

Rusty spins around. In the beam of his headlamp, Jeb is doubled over, laughing. "Knock it off, dude."

"Sorry, Vanisha," says Jeb. "It was too temptin' to pass up." He sweeps his hand around, motioning to the cave. "Cool, huh?"

"Cool," Rusty says.

"We oughta sleep here tonight. Bring our bags down. A pack of cards," says Jeb. "We could hang out."

"No way," I say.

It's one thing lying in the open woods, a few steps away from the safety of Jeb's truck. But sleeping here, in this creepy cave, would feel like being buried alive.

"Why not?" says Jeb. "It's clean. It's dry. It's safe."

"It's only safe till momma bear comes back," says Rusty. He shines his light on a gnawed bone lying in a corner.

That does it for me. "I'm out of here," I say.

"Aw, it's prob'ly just a possum," says Jeb.

But I don't care. I'm heading for the exit.

"C'mon, Jeb. You've freaked out Vanisha enough for today," says Rusty. "Let's get back to camp."

## chapter eight

Back at the campsite, we put up a tarp and start a fire from some dry wood we stashed under Jeb's truck. Rusty and I roast wieners on sticks. Jeb builds some kind of rack out of branches and duct tape to toast the hot dog buns over the fire.

"Dude, that's never gonna work," says Rusty.

"You be quiet," says Jeb, laying a bun on the rack. "I learned this here technique from my Cherokee ancestors."

"You don't have Cherokee ancestors," Rusty says.

"My great-great-grandpa was a Cherokee warrior," says Jeb. He makes a warrior face at Rusty. The rack collapses, dumping the bun into the fire.

"Your great-great-grandpa was a lunatic," says Rusty.

Jeb ignores him and shoves a hot dog on a stick to roast. "What're we gonna climb tomorrow?" he asks.

"Edge of Flight," I say.

Rusty nods, stuffing the end of a hot dog into his mouth.

"Jeepers, Vanisha," says Jeb. "I dunno how you pull that balancy stuff. I can't get more'n two feet up that climb."

"Ten years of ballet lessons," I say. "Comes in useful for some things."

"Seriously, Vanisha? You do ballet?" asks Rusty.

"Used to. I quit a couple of years ago."

"Why?"

Why? I bite into my hot dog. There were all the usual reasons—the hours of training,

47

the obsession over weight, the gossip and backstabbing. But it went beyond that. I didn't enjoy memorizing steps and performing them over and over and over again. There was no room to be creative or to think for myself.

That's one thing I love about climbing— each new route is a new puzzle to be solved. There is no single, right way to get from the bottom to the top. Like Chuck's Crack. The way Rusty climbed it was different from the way Jeb climbed it. The route taken depends on personal technique, strength and inspiration.

In climbing, too, there is the risk of a fall, which scares me to death but also draws me in. I feel this need to overcome it. To prove that I can. That's how it is when I stand at the crux of Edge of Flight. Part of me always wants to chicken out, but part of me says, *Do it, try it, risk it.* I want that second part to win. I want to train myself to be brave.

All that's too difficult to explain to the guys though.

"I guess I just got bored," I say instead. "Then I did cheerleading for a year."

"You were a cheerleader?" Jeb looks at me in disbelief, as if I'd just told him I was an invader from planet Zork. I stand up and throw a backflip to prove my cheer credentials.

Jeb whistles. "Wow, Vanisha. That's hot."

"Why'd you quit?" says Rusty.

"Don't even get me started."

"Bad?" says Rusty.

"Those girls can talk for hours about mascara and bra sizes," I say.

"Sounds great," says Jeb. "Where do I sign up?"

I'm about to give him a punch on the shoulder when a pair of headlights cuts through the woods. Car tires crunch to a stop on the dirt road next to our campsite.

Rusty shines his headlamp on the car. "It's the cops."

"Don't look at me," says Jeb. "I'm clean."

"You'd better be," says Rusty.

The deputy gets out of the car. He's wearing a heavy raincoat and a sour look on

49

his face, like he's not too pleased to be out patrolling the woods on a soaking-wet night. He comes up to stand by the campfire.

"You kids got a valid hunting license?" he says.

"We're not hunting, sir," says Rusty. "Rock climbing."

The deputy nods and walks around the fire. He makes a big deal of sniffing the air. All I can think of is how glad I am Jeb didn't take any of that weed.

"Y'all got any restricted materials in that there truck?" asks the deputy. "Alcohol? Fire arms? Illicit drugs?"

He draws out the last word, the way Southerners do for emphasis—"druuuuugs?" He glares at Rusty, Jeb and me.

"No, sir," says Jeb.

"Then y'all don't mind if I have a look." The deputy unhooks an enormous flashlight from his belt and opens the truck door.

Rusty shoots a look at Jeb, like, *Is he going to find anything?* Because we're in big trouble if he does. Arkansas isn't exactly known for being soft on crime.

But Jeb opens his hands wide and shakes his head, like, *I'm innocent. There's nothing there.*

Before today, I would have trusted Jeb without question. But his idiocy in the marijuana patch has shaken my confidence in him. What if he's got a stash of weed in his glove compartment, or hidden under a seat? What if he's got a couple of cans of beer hidden among all the junk in the back of the truck? Can we get charged with underage possession, even if we aren't drinking?

Would my mom have to come and pick me up at the police station? That would be embarassing. She'd probably go into a long rant about how bad the drinking laws are in America, and how Europeans have a much more sensible attitude, and how the ancient Greeks used to let their babies drink wine. She'd start quoting poetry. "A jug of wine, a book of verse, and thou..."

*Please, spare me.*

The deputy is definitely doing a thorough job of checking Jeb's truck. He rummages under seats and floor mats, hauls out mounds of stuff from the back.

He tosses them on the ground in a careless pile—CDs, sports magazines, sweatshirts, dirty socks, half-empty packs of gum, broken sunglasses, climbing rope, take-out burger wrappers, football gear.

No drugs. No booze.

Thank goodness.

After he's finished, the deputy comes back to stand at the campfire. He seems a little friendlier toward us.

"You play football?" he says to Jeb.

"Yessir," says Jeb. "Tight end."

"I'm a fan myself. Got season's tickets to the Razorbacks," says the deputy.

"Go, Pig, SOOOOOIEEEE!" Jeb hollers the Razorback cheer so loudly, it startles a flock of blackbirds from the trees.

The deputy almost cracks a smile. "Look, there's a mess of trouble you kids could get into up here. And I want y'all to stay out of it, you hear me?"

"Yessir," says Jeb.

"Just stick to your climbin', y'hear?"

"Yessir," Jeb says again.

Satisfied, the deputy leaves.

Nothing else happens that evening, except a lot of marshmallow-toasting and storytelling. But later on, as I snuggle into my sleeping bag for the night, I think back to Jeb's promise to stay out of trouble.

I hope he means to keep it.

## chapter nine

The rain tapers off and finally stops by midmorning, but it takes until afternoon before the hot Arkansas sun has burned the cliff face dry. At 3:00 PM, we rappel down the cliff and walk to the base of Edge of Flight.

"You ready?" Rusty asks.

I look up the arête—that perfect corner of rock that runs from the base to the top of the cliff. There's the crux—that smooth patch just below the pistol-hold grip. I pin my eyes to it, as though I could stare down the solid rock.

"I'm ready," I say.

"Commit to the move, Vanisha," says Rusty, as if he's read my mind about the crux. "You can do it. You've just got to commit."

I nod. "Right. I can do this."

I change into my climbing shoes and rope in, while Rusty sets the belay. Jeb, meanwhile, is wandering down the hiking trail that runs along the base of the cliff.

"Where are you going?" Rusty calls after him.

"Just takin' a li'l walk," Jeb says.

"Stay out of trouble!" Rusty shouts.

"Don't worry!"

*Trouble.* The same word the deputy used last night. It sets off a warning inside my brain. I want to call Jeb back. He's not wearing his orange hunting cap. It's not even stuck in his back pocket anymore. Rusty and I have ours on. I remember what the waitress said. *Some a them good ol' boys'll shoot at anything that moves.* I should give Jeb my cap. I won't need it for the climb.

But who am I, his mother? He would probably just laugh at me. I watch him walk into the woods, ducking branches and swatting mosquitoes.

"Don't bother about him, Vanisha," says Rusty. "Come on, let's climb."

I turn to face the cliff. I place my hands on the smooth sandstone, one on either side of the arête. I take a deep breath. All other thoughts go out of my mind. I am focused on Edge of Flight.

"Ready to climb," I say.

"On belay," says Rusty.

I reach up for the softball-shaped hold with my right hand. Stretch out my left and grip the arête. I place my right foot on the first microhold, slink my left foot around to find the other hold on the other side of the arête. Now I am perfectly balanced, straddling the corner of rock.

"Climbing," I say.

"Climb on," says Rusty. The next holds are vertical cracks—one on either side of the arête. I slide my right hand along the rock face until I feel a jagged gash. I shove my fingers inside. Good. A solid hold. My feet are solid too, though balanced on tiny footholds. Now it is safe to let go with my left hand and feel for the crack on that side. I find it and dig my fingers deep inside.

Legs are more important than arms on a climb. I know this, despite Jeb's show of brawn on Chuck's Crack yesterday. Legs are strong. Arms are weak. Arms tire out. Arms should be used for balance. Their strength should be saved for desperate moments or for strategic situations where there is no other choice.

My fingers hug the rock. But it is my feet that must do the work. I look down and scout for tiny footholds that will allow me to climb higher, one step at a time, while my hands inch their way up the vertical cracks.

After ten feet, I pause, balanced on two good footholds. So far, I have trusted the rock to support me. But now I am too high to climb unprotected. I need to lay some pro.

I let go with my right hand and unclip a small, metal nut from my harness. My left hand clenches the rock, while my right hand wedges the nut into the crack. I suppress a tremble in my legs. If I lose my balance before clipping in the rope, I will fall ten feet to the ground. I need to lay this pro for safety. But laying it is the trickiest part of climbing.

I wriggle the nut farther into the crack and give it a tug. It stays firmly stuck. I clip a carabiner into the metal wire on the nut and reach down for the rope. Its weight is heavy in my hand. My fingers shake, but I haul the rope up and clip it through the carabiner. The *click* of the 'biner closing sends a wave of relief through me.

"Looking good!" Rusty shouts up at me. I feel him tighten the belay. I stick my right hand back into the crack and lean against the rock for a moment to rest. For now, I am safe.

I can't stop for long though. Even staying still takes energy and strength. I have to keep moving. Five feet farther up, I lay another piece of pro in the right-hand crack. Then I traverse to the left side of the arête, where a series of small ledges and holes take me to just below the crux.

I lay one more piece of pro—a micronut in a tiny crack. Then I reach for the two handholds and step onto the nub of rock, the final foothold before the crux.

I am balanced on tiptoe on my right foot, my left leg crossed behind. My fingers prickle. My forearms burn. I have spent too much energy getting here already. I press my cheek against the rock and look up. The pistol-hold grip sticks out of the cliff face, far above. Too far above. The wind tears at my clothes. My heart beats against the rock.

"Commit, Vanisha!" Rusty shouts. "Commit!"

I straighten my left arm, lock the elbow, lean far to the right.

*Do it*, I tell myself. *Let go with your right hand. Do it. Do it.*

*I can't. What if I fall? What if the pro doesn't hold?*

*You can do it.*

*Commit.*

I let go.

And then a shotgun blast rips the air.

I jerk backward. I fall.

An incoherent scream bursts from my throat. I brace my hands forward as the rope catches me, and I swing against the rock face. My hands and feet cushion the jarring blow. I spring back. Swing toward the rock face again. Brace myself. Feel the shock of contact. Push off. Swing again. Finally, I'm dangling on the rope. Dizzy. Out of breath. But relieved. The pro held. I'm okay.

"Rusty? What's going on?"

Rusty is already belaying me down. He lets out the rope at breakneck speed, almost too fast to control my descent.

I twist in my harness to look behind me. Then I see Jeb running headlong through the woods, zigzagging through the trees, as if he's on the football field. He's trying to evade something. But what?

Another shot rings out. Jeb stumbles and crumples to the ground.

## chapter ten

As soon as I touch the ground, Rusty snaps the belay device off his harness and runs toward Jeb. I untie the rope from my harness, hands fumbling with the figure-eight knot. Somehow, I have the wit to tear the orange hunting cap off my head and grab Rusty's backpack from the ground. By this time, Rusty's got Jeb to his feet, and they're both running toward me. Jeb's leaning on Rusty hard, an arm draped over his shoulder.

"The Chimney!" Rusty's voice is urgent. I snatch the hunting cap off his head and fling it to the ground. Another gunshot splits the air. Behind us, men shout. Branches break. Heavy footfalls crash through the woods.

We reach the Chimney and drop to the ground. Rusty pushes Jeb ahead of him. I crawl through the entrance last, dragging Rusty's backpack behind me. There are drops of blood on the ground. We squeeze deeper into the Chimney.

I am about to start climbing it, but Rusty hisses, "No. Through here." He motions to the stone tunnel that leads to the secret cave. Jeb is rasping and heaving like a wounded animal. Somehow, Rusty pushes him through the stone tunnel. He makes it into the cave, where he collapses onto his stomach on the ground.

Jeb is groaning, but Rusty clamps a hand over his mouth to muffle the sound. Outside, the men are cursing, swearing. Their voices reach us faintly through the layers of rock.

*"Where'd they go...?"*

*"...hiding somewheres..."*

*"...must've went up the cliff..."*

*"...go up there and check it out..."*

The voices and footsteps move away until I can hear nothing from the outside. Inside the cave, it is miraculously still and silent. The air is cool and damp. We have reached sanctuary.

Jeb breathes in ragged, heavy pants. The air shaft at the end of the cave lets in just enough light to see by. I dig into Rusty's backpack, pull out his headlamp and first-aid kit. Rusty puts on the headlamp and rips Jeb's shirt off his back. A mess of blood covers Jeb's torso.

"Put some pressure on the wound, Vanisha," says Rusty.

I pull off my T-shirt, exposing my Lycra tank top underneath, and press it against the bloody smear on Jeb's back. I target my pressure on the hole where the bullet entered his flesh to stop the bleeding. Jeb moans in pain.

Rusty measures and cuts gauze bandages from his first-aid kit. He pours water from his Nalgene bottle on the wound, then cleans it with alcohol while Jeb winces.

"Dude, stay still," Rusty whispers, angry. "You went back there, didn't you?"

"Back where?"

"You know where," Rusty says.

"Aw, I just wanted to look around."

"That was stupid," Rusty says.

"Yeah," Jeb admits. "Stupid."

I help Rusty wrap bandages around Jeb's body. Somehow, we manage to get the bleeding under control. As we work, the cave begins to grow darker. The light from the air shaft dims. The cone of light from Rusty's headlamp becomes more and more distinct. In another hour or two, it will be all we have left to see by.

Rusty finishes taping up the dressing. Jeb's back is slick with sweat. His breath comes in shallow gasps.

"Lay still, dude," Rusty tells him. "Don't move. Don't talk. We're gonna get you out of this."

I squeeze Jeb's hand before Rusty and I move off to a corner of the cave. We need to talk where Jeb can't hear us.

"How bad is it?" I whisper.

Rusty shakes his head but doesn't answer.

"Worst-case scenario?" I say.

"Worst-case scenario, the bullet hit a major artery. But then, he'd already be dead."

"Okay. Second-worst-case scenario."

"I don't know, Vanisha. The bleeding's stopping, so that's good. But where did the bullet get him? It could've nicked the intestines. In which case..."

"In which case?"

"In which case, stuff starts oozing out. Infection sets in. If the infection gets into the bloodstream..."

"What?"

"It's bad."

"How bad?"

"He could die, Vanisha. He could die within twenty-four hours."

I look over at Jeb lying motionless on the ground. I'm worried about him, but I also feel like smacking him on the head. How could he have been so reckless?

"I'll get the truck and go for help," I say.

Rusty digs the keys and an extra headlamp out of his backpack. "My cell's in the glove box," he says. "As soon as you get a signal, call nine-one-one."

We hug without speaking, drawing strength from each other. Then I put on the headlamp and crawl out of the cave.

Inside the tunnel, the headlamp flickers. It's an old-model Petzl, the kind with the lightbulb instead of an LED. The contacts are wonky, so I have to twist it on just right. I reach up and tap it a couple of times, and the light steadies. It's not very bright, but the batteries are probably old. How long has Rusty owned this thing, I wonder. I should be thankful he even had a spare light.

I reach the bottom of the Chimney and stand. I'm still wearing my climbing shoes— my sneakers are lying at the base of Edge of Flight. The rubber soles grip the rock, giving me extra confidence in the dim light. As I get closer to the top, I hear men's voices.

They sound rough and rude—laughing and joking, but not in a friendly way. I turn off the headlamp. No use wasting the battery when there is still enough evening light to see by. No use signaling my presence either. I climb to the top and roll onto the ground. Keeping low. Keeping hidden.

Our campsite lies only a few dozen steps away. It's separated from me by a screen of bushes and slender trees. Flames roar in the fire pit. This is no cozy campfire. It's the kind of fire that signals destruction. Two men sit beside it, drinking beer and talking loudly. I can't make sense of what they're saying except that every second word is a curse. One of them stands up and swaggers toward Jeb's truck.

He's holding something in his hand. It looks like a short, heavy stick. He raises it and smashes it against the windshield. The glass shatters. The other guy laughs.

The first man raises his arm again. It's not a piece of wood he's holding, but a tire iron. He smashes it down on the hood of the truck. The dull, brutal *thunk* of metal crushing metal. He raises his arm again and again. Wrecking the truck. Destroying it. The flames leap. The man by the fire laughs. The air smells of smoke and cinders.

At last, I notice the patch on the back of the vandal's jacket. It's a picture of the Grim Reaper.

My heart clenches. Without making a noise, I slink down the Chimney to tell Rusty the bikers have taken over our campsite.

## chapter eleven

"Forget the truck," says Rusty. "Take the hiking trail back to town."

We're huddled in a dark corner of the cave. Safe, but not really safe. Jeb's rasping breath warns us we can't stay here long. We have to get out.

I know the hiking trail Rusty's talking about. It runs along the top of the cliff, then veers into the woods and winds its way down to Mount Judea, coming out at the river just before the bridge into town.

We walked it a couple of months ago. We were camping, and Jeb's truck battery died after he blasted the radio all night long. At the time, a dead truck battery seemed like a major disaster.

It will take an hour and a half, maybe two hours, to walk into town. But there's a problem. "That trail goes right through our campsite," I say.

"I know," says Rusty. "You'll have to pick up the trail farther down the bluff line."

"But the Chimney..."

"Forget about the Chimney, Vanisha. There's other ways up the cliff."

Suddenly, I know what he is thinking. Edge of Flight.

It makes sense. The route is a couple of hundred feet away. We could walk to it along the base of the cliff. Then I'd climb it and come out on top of the cliff at a spot way past our campsite. I could pick up the hiking trail and hike into town. The bikers wouldn't have a clue I had snuck past them.

Plus, the rope is still hanging there, unless the biker guys have trashed it. The pro is already laid for two-thirds of the route. It'll be an easy top-rope climb to the crux and—once I'm past the crux—a few simple moves over the chunky holds to the top.

But the crux.

"I don't know if I can pull it, Rusty."

"You have to, Vanisha."

"You could go..." I say.

But of course Rusty can't leave Jeb. Rusty's the one who knows first aid. He has to stay here to do whatever it takes to keep Jeb alive until help comes. I have to go.

"Okay," I say. "I'll do it."

It only takes Rusty a couple of minutes to check on Jeb and grab some gear from his backpack. We walk silently along the base of the cliff, anxiously watching the sun set and trying to reckon how many more minutes of daylight we have left to climb.

When we reach Edge of Flight, the rope is hanging exactly where we left it. My sneakers are lying in the dirt. I pick them up and clip them to my harness for the long walk into town. Then I rope myself in while Rusty sets the belay.

Without speaking, Rusty clips a couple of slings onto my harness. I'll need them to secure the rope in the handholds above the crux. I'm traveling light. No nuts, no hexes, no cams. The sound of metal gear clinking together could give us away to the bikers. I'm not wearing my headlamp either. But it's clipped to my harness in case of an emergency. Our best hope lies in silence and shadow.

I nod to Rusty, and he nods back. Then I step onto Edge of Flight.

I reach for the first holds more by memory than by sight. The fading sunlight washes away the texture of the rock. Sharp edges disappear. The surface of the sandstone is as blurry as an old black-and-white photograph. Deep breath. *Trust your instincts, Vanisha.*

The next handholds are the two vertical cracks. I run my hands along the surface of the rock, find the cracks and dig my fingers inside. Solid. Now for the footholds. That thing on the cliff below

my right knee looks like a rocky jag—
but my shoe scrapes and slides against the
bare cliff face when I try to stand on it.
Try again. Find the real foothold. Inch my
way farther up.

It's not pretty, this part of the climb.
But at least it's impossible to fall. The rope
is secured from above, and Rusty is holding
tight on belay.

But then comes the last piece of pro—
the last point where the rope loops through
a 'biner, holding me safe.

I pass beyond it. I am lead-climbing again.

And just above me lies the crux.

My hand grasps the nub of rock that
forms the only foothold in the crux. It is
smooth and solid, trustworthy. I rub it, hold
it, memorize its position in case my eyes fail
to find it again. Then it is time to let go, to
reach for the next set of handholds and step
up. Up to the nub of rock. Into the crux.

Balanced on one leg, I press my cheek
against the cliff face and look up. The pistol-
hold grip juts out from the rock above,

clearly visible even in the fading light. This is where I fell, only hours ago, jolted by the shotgun blast. But now, strangely, I feel no fear. My mind is calm and focused. There is no room for doubt. No room for hesitation. There is only one choice— to save Jeb's life.

My choice is already made.

I lock my left elbow, feel my forearm straining to hold on. I let go with my right hand and circle it upward in a smooth arc. I rise on my toes...balancing, balancing. I am at the tipping point. A shift of weight one inch the wrong way could cause me to swing out from the cliff, like a barn door swinging in a high wind. But I can't go back. I'm committed, committed to the move. The pistol-hold grip juts out of the rock above me. My fingertips brush against the sandstone. I can't quite grasp it. One more push with my trembling thigh muscles, a little higher on the tip of my toes. Yes. My hand reaches the pistol-hold grip. My fingers wrap around it. Now my left hand joins the right. A solid hold. I pull upward with all my might.

Slipping and scraping, my feet find no traction on the smooth rock face. Then I remember Jeb on Chuck's Crack, with his feet planted flat against the cliff. I lean back, straighten my arms, bend my knees and spring-load my thighs. I focus on the next big hold and push upward with all my might. Then I let go with my left hand and swing it upward. Yes! My fingers wrap around a rock handle. Solid. My right hand finds a jug. Bombproof.

My forearms are burning. But now I can raise a foot—raise it almost to shoulder height—and set it on the pistol-hold grip. My leg is bent almost double, my calf pressed against my hamstrings. I pull with my arm, push with my leg. My thigh shakes, but my leg slowly straightens until I am standing with one foot, and then two, on that solid pistol-hold grip. I hug the rock with my body, trembling with exhaustion and with relief.

There is no time to rest. I throw a sling over a jug of rock, clip in the rope with a 'biner and set a second sling for extra protection. To fall now, after achieving the crux, would be heartbreaking, unthinkable.

It's only a few feet to the top. I need to finish the climb before my energy runs out. Hand over hand, I bash my way from one huge hold to the next. Adrenaline courses through my body, charging me with courage.

Finally, the lip of the cliff. I grab two gnarly tree roots and haul myself over, squirming on my belly. On top of the cliff at last, I lie with my cheek pressed against the ground, gasping, panting, feeling my heart pound. A chorus of crickets fills the woods—the thrum of thousands of tiny voices. I flip onto my back and look at the sky. The first stars are coming out. The blue of night is beginning to replace the orange glow of sunset.

My mind goes back to Jeb. The bullet, the blood. *He could die within twenty-four hours.* I haul in the rope and coil it beside a tree. Down below, Rusty gives a final wave and heads back toward the cave.

I switch my tight climbing shoes for sneakers and take off my harness. The orange triangles nailed to the trees make the hiking trail easy to find. I set foot on the trail and take a deep breath. From here to Mount Judea, I am on my own.

## chapter twelve

Behind me, the bikers' campfire crackles. Its light flickers, but the men are nothing more than dark shapes among the trees. Their voices mingle with the sound of smashing glass. Are they still trashing the truck, or have they moved on to breaking beer bottles against rocks? I turn away and try to put them out of my mind. We've escaped them. Score one for us.

The trail runs along the bare rock of the clifftop. Twilight is fading quickly, but it's too risky to turn on my headlamp this close to the bikers. There is still enough light to see by.

A motorbike roars on the dirt roadway, and a headlight flashes through the woods. I freeze, but the headlight passes by. Is one of the bikers leaving, or are more arriving? I stumble on rocks and tree roots. There's no point in twisting an ankle. *Slow down, Vanisha.* But how long will it take to get to Mount Judea?

The trail veers from the edge of the cliff and leads into the woods. At first, the shapes of the trees remain visible. But after a few minutes of walking, the forest becomes nothing more than a dark blur. The trail is a grayish glow that cuts through the blackness on either side. I can't see more than a few feet ahead of me. At every step, the world around me grows a little darker. It is like walking in fog.

Another motorcycle roars down the road. I freeze, but the headlight flashes and disappears. The sound of the engine fades, and the forest seems darker than ever.

A pinpoint of light startles me. But it is only a firefly. Another firefly glimmers, then another, like the glitter of fairy light in the woods.

I step in what seems to be the direction of the trail, but find myself wading through tall grass and brambles. This can't be right. I turn on my headlamp. Suddenly, the shapes of the trees jump out—spindly branches and vines snaking around slender, crooked trunks. Something scurries in the underbrush. My chest clenches. Calm down. It's just some critters, as Jeb would say. Don't be a-skeered of the critters.

*Jeb.*

The headlamp's beam falls on an orange triangle marker on a tree. A few steps through the waist-high weeds take me back to the trail. But as I walk farther, the trail becomes narrower and narrower until it is not much more than a deer track through the woods. I turn off my headlamp. Pitch darkness—I cannot see my hand in front of my face. I fumble to turn it on again. Hopefully, the batteries will last. There is no way I can continue without light.

Crickets chirr. Mosquitoes bite my arms and legs. The sky darkens. The stars come out. I walk and I walk. I walk until I have no idea how long I've been walking or how far I've gone. Only the orange markers on the trees tell me I'm heading in the right direction. That, and the feeling of going downhill. Down, toward the river and the town. Down, toward help.

My headlamp flickers. A couple of sharp taps with my finger steady the beam. Are my eyes playing tricks on me, or is the beam growing dimmer?

*Crack!*

I stop in my tracks. It sounded like a branch breaking. I shine my headlamp around, but its beam shows only the black, spindly forms of trees and their weird shadows.

*Crack!*

I turn my headlamp off. If someone is coming, they must have a light. No one could find their way through the woods in this darkness. Rooted to the spot, I look around. There's no flashlight beam.

Maybe it's an animal? A deer? A bear? What else? Lynx, bobcat, cougar? Do they hunt at night? I crouch, trying to make myself invisible, and wait, my heart racing. Nothing happens. Seconds go by, then minutes. *If something were stalking me, it would have got me by now.* There's only one thing to do. Keep going, one foot in front of the other.

I twist the headlamp to turn it on, but no light appears. Panic throbs in my gut. *Breathe deeply. Calm down.* I fiddle with the headlamp. A light flickers. Flickers again. Then, a steady glow. Dimmer than before, but steady.

I take a few steps forward. The path seems to arc to the right. Around the bend, a warm, orange glow lights up a small patch of the woods. A campfire.

Another *crack!* sends a shower of sparks spinning and drifting toward the sky.

The path leads past the campfire. In the firelight, the dark shapes of people move around the small clearing. Mellow voices thrum through the darkness. Hunters.

A couple of the good ol' boys, as the waitress in the diner would say.

Their campsite is not far off the trail—maybe fifty or seventy-five feet through the woods. Why not run over there and ask them for help?

A burst of laughter, deep-throated. Their voices are garbled. How many men are there? Two? Three? More?

What if they're drunk? What if one of them grabs me?

*It won't happen, Vanisha.* But they're complete strangers. I'm a girl, alone, in the night. In the middle of nowhere. It's not safe. Jeb already got us into trouble messing around where he didn't belong.

I have to be careful—for my sake, and for Jeb's. I'm Jeb's only hope. I have to protect myself.

My quiet footsteps take me past the campsite and beyond, farther into the woods. In less than a minute, the light of the campfire and the sound of voices have disappeared. I run for as long as I can and then walk. I am surrounded by the chirring of insects, the rustling underbrush, and sometimes the roar of an engine on the unseen road. I walk so far, I begin to second-guess myself. I should have stopped. I should have asked for help.

It's too late now.

My headlamp grows dimmer and dimmer until at last the battery dies. No amount of fiddling will coax a light out of the dark bulb.

I stand stock-still. It's critical not to get turned around and lose my place on the trail. Overhead, the treetops make black patterns against the glowing night sky. There are thousands of stars, but no moon. Maybe I should sit down and wait for it to rise. It will be full tonight. Maybe it will cast enough light for me to see my way.

But how much time will I lose if I wait? One hour? Two? Hours that might be critical to Jeb.

I close my eyes. The woods are so black, it makes no difference whether my eyes are open or closed. But closing them helps me focus. I hear the sigh of my breath, my pulse hammering in my eardrums and the sustained note of cricket song. But beneath those sounds, there's a low, steady, undercurrent of rushing water. The river. It must be close by. If I find the riverbank, I can follow it to the bridge and take the road into town. I might even be able to see the lights of Mount Judea on the opposite bank.

I take a step forward. A tree branch hits me in the face. Am I going in the right direction? Now that I can hear the rushing water, the sound seems to surround me. I take a few more steps. Weeds as tall as my thighs brush against my legs. This is hopeless. Surely I've lost the trail.

Then I see a light.

A firefly, I think at first. It is bright and white, not flickering orange like a campfire. But my eyes are playing tricks on me. The light is far away and much bigger than a firefly's glow. It doesn't float and disappear. It stays steady, like a cabin's porch light, maybe. A stranger's cabin. This time, I am ready to throw myself on the kindness of strangers.

Brambles scrape my legs. I hold my hands in front of me to push away tree branches. Every step closer makes the light more distinct—not one light, but two. Not a cabin, but a pair of headlights from a car parked on the road.

The rushing water is louder now. The river must be close. That means the bridge into town is close.

I creep to the edge of the road and peek out from the cover of dense bushes.

A car door slams. A man walks in front of the headlights. He is tall and lean, with a gun at his waist and a ranger-style hat on his head.

It's the deputy.

Thank goodness.

I step onto the road.

## chapter thirteen

I am about to call out to him when something makes me freeze. There is a second figure in the shadows behind the cruiser's headlights. My jaw clenches. My voice dies in my throat. It's a big, burly man with black hair and a beard. And he's straddling a motorcycle.

The biker dismounts and swaggers toward the deputy. As he walks in front of the headlights, I see his face—the same man who trashed Jeb's truck. He slaps the deputy on the shoulder in a friendly way, and the deputy laughs. Then the biker hands him a package. At that moment, I know the package contains one of two things. Money or drugs.

I take a step backward. A twig cracks beneath my foot. The men's heads turn in my direction.

"Hey!" the deputy shouts. "Hey, you!"

He runs toward me. But I dodge into the woods, keeping close to the side of the road, where there is just enough light to see by. My feet feel light and swift. I duck under branches and deke around trees, past the cruiser, past the motorbike. Then I dart back onto the road, where the ground is smoother. I feel like a track-and-field runner. Fast. Sure-footed. My arms pump. My feet fly over the dirt road. It slopes downward, and I pick up speed. I feel as though nothing can stop me. I round a bend in the road. The forest ends, not far ahead of me. I see the river and the bridge into town.

An engine roars. I leap back into the woods and thrash through the underbrush.

Brambles tear at my clothes, but I know it is not far now—not far to the river, to the town and to help.

Who can I ask for help, if the deputy is friends with the bikers' gang? I don't know. I just know I have to get there.

I climb a steep rise, panting and choking on my breath. Suddenly the woods open up, and the hiking trail appears again at the edge of a steep drop. Fifteen feet below the river rushes a mass of frothing, churning white water.

I grab a tree branch to stop myself from pitching forward. The ground is muddy from the river spray and the rain. Across the river, the lights of Mount Judea shine, and the full moon rises, at last, above the trees. On my right, only fifty feet downriver, is the bridge.

There is no time to waste. The deputy is thrashing through the woods behind me. I turn and run, my feet slipping and sliding in the mud. But as I approach the bridge, I see the form of a man straddling a motorcycle. The biker is blocking the way across.

I spin around. My foot catches on a root in the mud. I fall headfirst, pitching over the embankment. My hands grapple for a hold and find a thick tree root. Sobbing and panting, I cling to it. My cheek presses against the ravine. White water sprays against my legs.

Above me, I hear the deputy shout, "Hey, you! Hey, kid! C'mon out here!"

*It's time to give up, Vanisha. It's time to beg for help.* How long can I hold on to this root? And even if I can hold on until he leaves, will I be able to pull myself back up?

The deputy will save me, won't he? He's a law-enforcement officer. I'll promise not to rat him out. I'll say I didn't see anything. I'll promise...but what about Jeb? If I tell the deputy where Jeb is, how do I know he won't tell the bikers? How do I know he won't let them have their revenge? No, I can't risk trusting the deputy.

Below, the river froths and boils. To my left, a gnarly shrub grows at the base of the ravine, near the water's edge. It's not far. A couple of good bouldering moves would take me there. If only I could find a foothold.

I probe with my feet along the rock face. There's a pocket to shove my right foot into, and a solid ledge for my left. I ease my weight onto my legs and feel the relief in my arms. My target is in sight.

A large rock sticks out of the cliff to my left. I try it as a handhold. It's damp but solid. Letting go of my trusty root, I match hands, match feet, and slide myself sideways across the rock face. So far, so good.

I slink my left hand along the rock wall, searching for another hold. A rock juts from the cliff face, but it is smooth and wet, too slippery to hold. Above it, my fingers dig into a deep rock pocket. I tug down. It's good and solid. Now for the next foothold.

*Ignore the rushing river. Focus on finding a hold.* A rock sticks out like a stepping-stone. I pose my left foot on it, gently. It seems solid. I begin to shift my weight. But the rock breaks off beneath my foot. My leg flails in the air. I grip the cliff face tighter and hug my body against it.

91

My heart pounds. My pulse throbs in my throat. I breathe deeply. *Get control. Everything's okay.* My left foot taps along the rock face until it finds another place to stand. A smaller foothold, but solid. Gradually, I shift my weight onto it. It holds. I take a deep breath, refocus, match hands, match feet. One more lateral move takes me directly above the gnarly shrub.

I crouch and reach one leg down into the basket formed by the shrub's thick, tough branches. I set my foot on the base of the trunk that grows out of the rock. Bombproof, as Jeb would say.

*Jeb.*

I reach the other foot down. The trunk holds. My stance is steady. I lower my body into the shelter of the branches. Tucked into a ball, at last I feel safe.

The white noise of the river rushes below. But from above come the voices of the deputy and the biker.

"You see where she went?" asks the deputy.

"Must've run off in the woods somewheres."

"You catch a good look at her face?"

"Couldn't see. Too dark."

"Looked like a high school kid."

"Yeah. Prob'ly a bush party. Underage drinkin'."

"Makin' out with her boyfriend."

Laughter.

"How much d'you reckon she saw?" says the deputy.

"Nothin' that'd hold up in court. Like I said, too dark."

A flashlight casts a search beam down the ravine.

"I sure hope she didn't go over."

"That's one way to get rid of a witness, deputy," says the biker and laughs.

"Don't even joke about that."

"That's three miles of white water right there. If she fell into that, she ain't comin' out alive."

The flashlight's beam sweeps over the water again.

"Nah. She's run off into the woods," says the deputy.

"A course she did, deputy."

"She'll find her friends and be safe 'n' sound back in town by tomorrow morning."

"A course she will."

"Been a long night."

"C'mon up to my campsite, deputy. I got somethin' that'll make you forget your troubles."

The flashlight beam sweeps down the ravine one more time, then disappears along with the voices. I am alone and shaking with exhaustion and betrayal. How can an officer of the law leave a kid lost and alone in the woods? What if I had fallen into the river and died?

It takes a few minutes to steady myself before I can confront my next problem. How am I going to get out of here?

## chapter fourteen

Straight up. That's my first thought. Fifteen feet to the top of the ravine, then find a root or branch or something to haul myself over the top. If I fall, maybe the bush will stop me from tumbling into the river. Maybe. But is there a scalable route to the top? It's impossible to tell from here.

I could traverse back the way I came. At least I know there are handholds and footholds. But will I be able to find them again? It's a longer route than climbing straight up. And if I fall, there is nothing to catch me.

I'd rather head toward the bridge than away from it. It's a simple bridge—flat, with a metal trellis that supports it from below. If I were standing on a raft on the river, I could grab the lower beams and swing myself up. Then I could shinny up the trellis. But a raft isn't an option. Maybe there's another way to reach the underside.

Maybe I could find enough handholds and footholds to boulder across to the rock wall to my left and reach the bridge. But that's risky. There is one other possible route. A huge, sun-bleached driftwood log lies in the water along the river's edge. It's caught between the boulders of the riverbed and the rock wall of the ravine. The water licks around it but doesn't flow over it. If I use it as a balance beam, maybe I can reach the underside of the bridge.

But if I fall off the log into the river— *that's three miles of white water right there.* I'll be careful. I won't fall. Of all the options, it is my best chance.

I ease myself out of the bush and crouch on the log. I don't dare to walk on its slippery surface. So I lie on my belly and straddle it. I grip it between my knees and plunge my arms and legs into the cold water.

Broken-off stubs of branches stick out of the log. I grab them and pull myself forward until I'm beneath the bridge. The metal trellis hangs less than six feet above me. *Almost there.*

Carefully, I draw my legs underneath me. Water squelches in my sneakers. Holding tight to the stub of a branch, I try to plant my feet on the log and stand. But I have barely reached a crouch when my left foot slips and plunges into the fast-moving water. I grab the log, lying flat on my belly once again. The bridge hovers above. If only I could stand up.

Ahead, a boulder juts out of the river like an island. The current parts around it, rushing and swirling. Its rough surface looks better for traction than the slick log. I inch forward until I come alongside it. But there is a foot-wide gap between the log and the rock. I reach across the gap with my left arm, fingers clutching the stone. My chest plunges into the icy water. The current rips at my body, trying to drag me downriver.

*Ignore it. Focus on the next move. Commit.*

Now the left leg. I swing it over to straddle the rock. My body hangs like a sagging suspension bridge between the rock and the log. *Let go of the log. There's no other option. Commit.* The river yanks at me. But I fight it, swing my right hand like a grappling hook at the rock and grab it. My right leg dangles in the current like a piece of driftwood. I heave my leg out of the water. Hunkered on the rock, gasping, I raise my head to look up at the bridge.

The sound of rushing water thunders in my ears. I slowly rise from my crouch. Every inch toward standing is an effort of balance. The water rushes dizzyingly around me. But I focus on my goal—the solid metal beam of the bridge. Stretching up, I at last touch it and grab hold with both hands.

I wish I had Jeb's strength to hoist myself chin-up style to the lower beam of the bridge.

But Rusty taught me raw strength isn't everything. There's always another way. I swing my legs and plant my feet against the rock wall of the ravine. A few steps up the wall take me to horizontal. I kick my legs and wrap them around the beam. For a moment, I hang there upside down. Then I hoist myself over to lie on the beam facedown. My wet clothes cling to my skin. The metal smells like rust, like blood.

A trellis of diagonal struts joins the metal beam to the roadway above. Squirming up one of the struts, I grab the bridge's metal railing and pull myself higher until my head reaches the level of the roadway. I haul one leg onto the surface of the bridge. Dirt and pebbles scrape against my belly as I drag the rest of my body over.

The full moon shines on the empty road. The water below the bridge sounds faraway, now that I've escaped it. Rusty would have been faster and more agile. Jeb would have been stronger. But I did it. I made it to town. I saved myself.

Now I need to save Jeb.

## chapter fifteen

Water squelches from my sneakers with every step on the road into Mount Judea. My clothes hang from my body in sopping clumps. Main Street is shut down for the night. There's no light on at the gas station or the general store. The diner's empty, and the sign on its door is turned to *Closed*. But a light burns at the back of the building. The waitress stands outside, leaning against the brick wall, drinking a cup of coffee. The door to the diner's kitchen is propped open with a chair. Light and the sound of a radio playing country music come from inside the kitchen.

Even after a full day's work, the waitress still looks dolled up, with her blond hair pinned in a perfect bun. I comb my fingers through my wet tangles and walk toward her. I'm ready to ask for help anywhere I can find it.

"Honey, what happened to you?" Her black mascara makes her eyes pop wide.

"I need help," I say.

"Why, you're the girl that was goin' out climbin' with them boys from the city," she says. "Now before you say anything, you need somethin' dry on your back and somethin' warm in your belly."

She takes my arm and hustles me into the kitchen. The bright fluorescent lights are blinding after my long trek through the dark. The ceramic tile floor shines. The stainless-steel counters gleam. Every pot, pan, knife and spatula hangs in its proper place. I blink and squint while the waitress opens a closet door and pulls out a sweatshirt.

"Take your top off, honey. Don't be shy. I got kids. I seen it all. Now put this on. That's right, and sit down whiles I git you somethin' to eat."

She bustles around, laying food in front of me—steaming chicken and grits, pecan pie, hot coffee. My hand shakes as I pick up the fork. Once I start eating, I can't stop until it's all gone. The waitress pulls up a stool beside me.

"You look like you're in a mess of trouble, honey. Why don't you tell me what's goin' on?"

The whole story comes rushing out of me. Jeb snooping around in the marijuana patch, the bikers chasing us, the gunshot wound, the truck getting trashed, the deputy and his dealings with the bikers.

"We need to get Jeb to a hospital. But how can we do that, if the deputy's on the side of the bikers?" I ask.

The waitress taps her long red fingernails against her coffee cup. "I never did trust that deputy," she says. "Them boys was dealin' so much drugs right under his nose, you had to figure he was either dumb as a mule or he was in on it."

She takes a sip of coffee. "Well, there's the volunteer fire department, but it's run by the deputy's brother, so that's out. Then there's the state troopers, but they're an hour away, and the first thing they'll do is call the sheriff's office. If the deputy's in on it, could be the sheriff's in on it too."

"What about calling the hospital? We could get them to send an ambulance," I say.

"Honey, as soon as you call the hospital with a story like that, they're gonna call the police and the fire department. Emergency responders. Y'see? It'll go right back to the sheriff and his deputy. You want anything official done around here, it goes right back to the sheriff's office. Everything."

"So what does that leave?" I ask, my spirits sinking.

"That leaves nothing much else but us," she says.

"Us?"

"Yep," she says. "Us."

The waitress whisks my plates off the counter and washes them.

"What did you say your name was, hon?" she asks, drying her hands on a dishtowel.

"Vanisha."

She takes my hand and squeezes it tight, as a mother would. Although, she's about the furthest thing from my own mother I could possibly imagine.

"I'm Loretta. Best waitress in Newton County," she says. "And more than just a pretty face."

She opens the closet again, trades her high heels for a pair of sneakers and takes a large leather purse off a hook. "Tell me again what them bikers looked like," she says.

I describe the big, burly guy with the Grim Reaper on his jacket. She nods. "That's Shank. Who else?"

"The other guy had black hair in a ponytail and tattoos all down his arms."

"They call him Blade. Is that it?"

"That's all I saw."

Loretta walks over to the refrigerator, pulls out a jug of amber liquid and pours some into an unmarked glass bottle. She closes the bottle with a screw cap.

"What are you going to do?" I ask.

"Honey, if I know them boys, they're half drunk and stoned already. They'll pass out eventually. I'm just gonna help them along with a little home brew and Southern charm."

She pops the bottle into her purse.

"So, we're going to put them to sleep?" I ask. It doesn't sound like a foolproof plan.

"That's right, honey. Neutralize the enemy. Then we can go on in and rescue your friend."

She pulls something else out of her purse. It looks like a pen, or a miniature flashlight. She tucks it into her hair so it's hidden in the curls of her updo.

"Itty-bitty camera," she says before I have time to ask. "I been usin' it to spy on my girlfriend's no-good, cheatin' husband. Looks like it'll come in handy again."

"What for?"

"Honey, if we're gonna nail the deputy, we're gonna need some proof."

"Nail the deputy?" I say.

"Sure. You said he was corrupt, didn't you? Let's go in there and get some evidence."

"I don't want to nail the deputy. I just want to get Jeb to a hospital."

Loretta waves her hand. Her red fingernails flash like warning signs. "Come on now, honey. Might as well kill two birds with one stone."

# chapter sixteen

Driving through the woods in Loretta's truck, I can't stop worrying about Jeb. *Hang tight*, I tell him in my head. *We're coming.*

I try not to doubt Loretta and her Southern-charm plan. Maybe she's right. Maybe these guys will just drink themselves into oblivion and we can waltz in under their noses and rescue Jeb from the cave.

What other choice do we have anyway? Gather a posse of hunters and go in there, guns blazing? That's a sure way to get someone shot and killed.

As we round the last switchback before our campsite, Loretta tells me to climb over the seats and hide on the floor in the back.

"There's a blanket back there some-wheres," she says. "Git under it. We don't want them boys to see you."

I cram myself onto the floor below the truck's tiny backseat. Something hard and lumpy digs into my ribs. I pull it out from under me. It's a locked rifle case. Somehow, it's reassuring to know Loretta has protection. Still, how much use is a rifle, locked and stowed in the truck, if things start to go wrong? I slide it onto the backseat, then pull down the blanket and huddle beneath it on the floor.

"No matter what happens, you stay there till I come and git you," Loretta says. "Remember, I know them boys, and they all know me. I know how to handle 'em. You don't."

Those are her last words. A few minutes later, the truck jolts to a stop, and I feel the driver's door open, then slam shut.

"Why, deputy!" The waitress's voice sounds high and cheerful. Flirty. "You're surely makin' it a late night."

"Loretta," comes the voice of the deputy. "What brings you out here?"

His voice sounds defensive. Guilty. Like someone who's been caught shoplifting a chocolate bar and tries to hide it behind his back.

Loretta's voice is warm and sweet as honey. "My brother's got a huntin' camp a little ways farther on. I was fixin' to visit him, and then I spotted y'all. And I said to myself, them boys look like they could do with a little company."

"We surely could, Loretta. What's that you've got there in the bottle?" asks the deputy.

"A little brew of my own, Jim. Care for a taste?"

"Don't mind if I do..."

The banter continues. Loretta's voice, the deputy's, and the voices of two bikers, Shank and Blade. Loretta's Southern-charm offensive seems to go on for hours. Lying beneath the blanket, I drift in and out of sleep. Bits of conversation and laughter mix in my head with nightmares of dark caves, blood-soaked wounds and Jeb moaning in pain.

Finally, the *click* of the truck door wakes me up.

"Vanisha," Loretta whispers.

I sit up. "What happened?"

"They're stone-cold drunk and sleepin' like babies," she whispers. "Let's go find your friend."

My legs prickle with pins and needles as I uncurl from beneath the blanket and step out. Jeb's truck looks like something hauled out of a junkyard. The windows are smashed, the doors are bashed in, the tires are slashed and the hood is dented in a dozen places.

"Hope your friend's in better shape than his truck," Loretta whispers.

"I hope so too."

The campfire has died down to a pile of charred embers and a few glowing logs. The two bikers are snoring on either side of it, lying on our sleeping mats. They must have stolen them from the back of the truck. The deputy, who obviously wasn't planning to stay the night, is passed out on the ground with his back propped against a tree stump.

"Did you get your evidence?" I whisper to Loretta.

"Caught the deputy-sheriff on video, smokin' a joint with them bikers. Wait till I hand that over to the state troopers."

I grab a flashlight from Loretta's jeep and run to the top of Edge of Flight to retrieve the rope and my climbing harness. We drive the jeep a little farther away, so that if the men wake up, they'll think Loretta's gone. And we can evacuate Jeb without having to pass through the campsite again.

"Do you know how to rappel?" I ask as we pick our way through the woods toward the Chimney.

"Honey, I spent my whole life tryin' to attract men, not repel 'em," she says.

"No, I mean like rappel down a rope."

"Honey, I don't even know what that means."

We arrive at the Chimney, a dark gash in the earth. I shine the flashlight down it. The rock walls seem to close in like a trap. Anything could be lurking inside. Snakes, spiders, rats.

Loretta takes one look and steps away, shaking her head. "I don't think so, hon."

"It's not that bad," I say. "Besides, that's where Jeb is."

"Down there?"

"Yeah. That's where the cave is."

I unclip a couple of slings from my harness and wrap them around the trunks of two trees close to the Chimney entrance. I gather the slings together and clip two 'biners onto them. Two trees, two slings, two 'biners. If one fails, the other will hold. Then I clip the rope into the 'biners and throw both ends of the rope down the Chimney. Now we've got a top rope to rappel down. In this darkness, it's safer than free-climbing. Besides, we'll need the rope to evacuate Jeb. I turn to Loretta. "Ready?"

She shakes her head.

"You can use my harness," I say. "I'll show you how."

Loretta looks down the black hole of the Chimney like she's trying to work up her nerve. She backs away and shakes her head again. "Sorry, hon. I'll wait for y'all in the truck."

She hugs me and disappears from sight amid the trees. In the woods, especially at night, people vanish before you even realize they're gone. It's creepy. Something could be right behind you, and you wouldn't even know it was there.

I put that thought out of my head. There's no point worrying about imaginary danger, when Jeb's danger is real enough. I fasten my harness around my waist, loop the double-rope into my belay device and lower myself over the edge of the Chimney. The flashlight hangs from my harness, its beam jerking and dancing as I descend through the familiar sandstone crack. In the deeper reaches of the Chimney, the moonlight becomes fainter and fainter. I'm forced to rely on the flashlight, touch and memory. The rope holds me safe over boulders and into narrow, rocky gaps. Finally I land on the soft, sandy ground.

A voice, moaning and muttering, comes from inside the cliff. Hope makes my heart beat faster. *Jeb. He's still alive.*

I unclip the rope, drop to my knees and shine the flashlight around the Chimney, to locate the stone tunnel. At the end of the tunnel, Rusty is waiting for me in the cave. He picks me up and holds me tight against him. My head presses into his chest. His clothes smell of sweat and dirt, but his strong arms feel good. I lean against him, soaking in his warmth and strength.

"You made it," he says. "Did you get help?"

"She's waiting outside in a truck."

"She? Who's she?" Rusty relaxes his arms, and I step back.

"It's a long story, Rusty." I tell him the gist of it as quickly as I can.

"So we've got to get Jeb out of here on our own?"

"Yeah," I say. "How is he?"

"He's bad."

I kneel beside Jeb and take his hand. It feels cold and clammy, yet his forehead, when I touch it, burns. His body shudders. He groans and mumbles something about football.

I stand up and turn back to Rusty. "We can get him out of here. Right?"

"Right," says Rusty. "We're going to have to."

## chapter seventeen

"We need a stretcher," says Rusty. "Where's the rope?"

"I left it hanging in the Chimney."

"Good. Go get it."

Back in the Chimney, the ends of the rope dangle, just touching the sandy ground. From the woods, the night song of crickets filters down, but no human sounds, no voices—no hint the bikers have woken up. The rope drops down with a smooth pull, and I crawl back into the cave with it.

"Great," says Rusty. "Help me lay it out."

We lay the rope out on the ground in a zigzag so it makes the shape of a rectangular mat big enough for Jeb to lie on. When we've finished, several yards of rope are left over. Rusty takes the slack end and threads it back through the zigzag, tying knots with it as he goes. Finally, he ends up with a row of loops along each side of the mat.

"Now we need a couple of long branches," he says. "We thread the branches through the loops, here, and they become the poles on either side of the stretcher."

"And Jeb lies in the middle?" I ask.

"Right. Like a hammock."

"Smart."

"Wilderness Rescue 101," says Rusty. "Come on. Let's go find some branches."

He checks Jeb's pulse before we leave. He shakes his head and gives Jeb a drink of water. Then he shoulders his backpack and puts on his headlamp. We leave the flashlight with Jeb, its beam casting a circle of light on the cave's ceiling. At least he won't be alone in the dark. Where there's light, there's hope.

"We'll be right back, buddy," Rusty says. "Hang in there. We're getting you out of here."

At the base of the cliff, the full moon shines on the pale sandstone rock face. Our footsteps break the stillness, snapping twigs and crackling through fallen leaves. We soon come to an old, fallen tree. But the rotten wood crumbles in our hands. We find another one, but the branches are dry and brittle. Good campfire wood, but it would snap under Jeb's weight. Time is wasting. Our window of opportunity to get Jeb out alive is shrinking.

"Here." Rusty sets down his backpack at the base of a skinny tree. "We'll cut down these saplings. This one and that one just over there."

He reaches into his backpack and pulls out a folding saw. It looks like a jackknife, only bigger, with jagged teeth on the blade.

"Have you got everything in that backpack?" I ask him.

"Pretty near."

We saw down the two little trees and cut off their branches to make two eight-foot-long poles. Back in the cave, it doesn't take long to thread the poles through the loops on either side of Rusty's homemade stretcher. He tightens the knots on the loops so the poles are tied firmly in place. He takes two smaller branches and ties them crosswise at the head and foot of the stretcher to create a stable frame. We roll Jeb on his side and place the stretcher underneath him, then roll him back onto it. He groans. Rusty takes some thick webbing out of his backpack and ties Jeb to the stretcher.

"Ready?" Rusty says.

"Ready," I say.

Together, we push and drag Jeb through the tunnel, until we reach the bottom of the Chimney.

Rusty shines his headlamp on the first tumbled-down boulder. I scramble on top of it.

"I'll lift the front of the stretcher up to you, and you grab it," he says. "You pull up, and I'll push from the back."

Rusty manages to tilt the stretcher so it's leaning against the boulder. I reach down and grab the poles, but I can't budge them. My knuckles scrape painfully against the rock. Rusty pushes from below.

"Just lift it up a bit, Vanisha. So it's not right against the rock."

"I can't."

"Yes, you can. If you lift it so it's not rubbing, I can push it up."

I look down at Jeb's face, pale and sweating. I will myself to find the strength. But I can't lift the stretcher one inch.

"I can't do it, Rusty."

"Yes, you can, Vanisha. You have to."

"If we had some rope..."

If we had an extra rope, I realize, we could tie it to the stretcher, run it through a carabiner at the top of the Chimney and create a pulley system. In fact, the slings and carabiners I set up when I rappelled down the Chimney are still hanging there. With a pulley, it would be easy to hoist Jeb's weight. If we had a rope...

"There's an extra rope in the truck," Rusty says after I tell him my idea.

Fear makes me hesitate, but only for a moment.

"Okay, I'll go get it."

With Rusty's headlamp, it's easy to climb the Chimney. Adrenaline and guilt drive me forward. I feel guilty for not being strong enough to lift Jeb. For failing to bring a better rescue team. If I'd asked the hunters in the woods for help, we'd probably have Jeb safely to the hospital by now. Instead, he's stuck at the bottom of a crevice, and our emergency evacuation team is a waitress in a pickup truck.

What was I thinking?

At the top of the Chimney, I pause but don't see or hear anything suspicious. A few quiet steps along the trail take me to our campsite. The bikers and the deputy are still slumbering around the remains of the campfire. I keep to the edge of the clearing, ready to duck into the woods if one of them wakes. But the men don't stir.

I creep around to the back of the truck, turn the handle and open the hatch. As it swings up, pieces of glass from the shattered windowpane fall in a shower into the back of the truck. I crawl over them carefully and reach back to close the hatch in case someone wakes.

The inside of the truck is a mess of clothes, sleeping bags, backpacks—all the stuff the deputy pulled out during his search and we tossed back without bothering to sort it. Glass shards cover everything. I crouch, not wanting to kneel on a splinter, take off my headlamp and shine it around, keeping the beam low so it won't be visible outside.

A red sock lies in a corner. I pick it up carefully, using my thumb and index finger as tweezers, and shake it to get rid of the glass sticking to the outside. It's a thick wool hiking sock. It's a little crusty on the inside, but that's the least of my worries. I pull it over my hand so I can search for the rope without getting cut.

I sift through sweatshirts, football magazines, nylon stuff sacks. It's got to be here somewhere. Finally, through the muffle of the wool sock, I feel the bumpy ridges of a coiled rope. I yank it out from under the heap. The rope is beautifully coiled and tied. Probably Rusty's work. Jeb would have left it in a tangle. I sling it over my shoulder and crab-walk to the hatch door. But just as I'm about to open it, a bulky shape rises beside the campfire.

One of the men is getting up.

I shut off my headlamp and duck down. *Lie flat*, I tell myself. But the glass shards are everywhere. I huddle in a ball, arms crossed over my face.

The man stumbles toward the truck. He's singing a Johnny Cash song. "I shot a man in Reno just to watch him die..."

Oh god.

I squeeze myself tighter into a ball, shut my eyes. *Please don't open the truck.* What would I do if he did? Nothing. Stay still. No. I would jump down and make a run for it.

Something rustles outside. It sounds like water trickling from a hose.

He's pissing against the truck.

I'd laugh, if I wasn't so terrified.

Eventually, the biker stumbles back to bed. I count to five hundred to make sure he's asleep, grab the rope and run back to Rusty.

## chapter eighteen

We set up the pulley system as planned, tying the rope to Jeb's stretcher, then threading it up the Chimney, through the carabiners at the top and back down to the ledge eight feet below the Chimney's opening. As an extra safety measure, we anchor a GRIGRI to the ledge and thread the rope through it. The GRIGRI's a kind of belay device that will lock the rope in place, even if I accidentally let go. I take my position on the ledge and give Rusty a nod.

We've agreed not to speak for fear of waking the bikers. He disappears down the chimney, and I'm left with no company but the full moon shining through the lattice of tree branches.

Waiting for Rusty's signal to begin pulling, I can't help remembering my thoughts when Jeb first discovered the cave. *Sleeping there would feel like being buried alive in a tomb.* It could have become a tomb for Jeb if the bullet had hit an artery. If he had bled to death. If I had fallen into the river. If I had failed to return with help. It could still become a tomb, I think. But I push the thought away. Somehow, we'll get out of this. Somehow, we'll claw, scrape and scratch our way out of the darkness, into the light. Out of the underworld, into the land of the living.

The rope jerks three times—Rusty's signal to start the evacuation. I pull on the rope and feel the weight of Jeb's stretcher inching upward. I want to shout in excitement and relief. I want to call down to Rusty, "It's working!"

But we can't risk waking the bikers.

I pull on the rope, and the stretcher rises, inch by inch, foot by foot. Every gain is locked in place by the GRIGRI. Then there's a pause, and the rope goes slack. Rusty must have reached a ledge and stopped for a break. I shake out my hands and let the GRIGRI hold the rope. Overhead, the treetops make dark, intricate shapes against the sky.

I shine my flashlight down the Chimney but can't see Rusty and Jeb. It's not a straight route but a twisty, dodgy course through the spaces between fallen boulders and rock walls. Three tugs signal it's time to get to work again. I tighten the rope and haul in. Another few inches gained. Slowly, the stretcher jerks upward. We're making good progress. Any moment, I expect to see the poles of the stretcher peek over the rock ledge. But then everything stalls. I yank on the rope. It won't budge. Maybe Rusty's resting again. But the rope is taut, not slack. It doesn't feel like a rest stop. I shine my flashlight down the Chimney again but see only gray boulders, jagged rock slabs and shadows. No glimpse of Rusty and Jeb.

"Vanisha?"

It's startling to hear Rusty's voice after we'd agreed to work in silence.

"Rusty?"

"Come down. It's stuck."

Stuck? I glance nervously upward, wishing I could see the campsite. But there's nothing but the black silhouettes of trees against the sky. Carefully, I ease my grip on the rope. The GRIGRI clamps shut, holding it tight. I lay my flashlight on the rock ledge and lower myself halfway over the edge, feeling for footholds.

If I jam one foot on the wall behind me, I can push the other against the wall in front of me—positioned like a runner clearing a hurdle. There's a good handhold on the underside of the ledge. I fumble around with my left hand until I find the scooped-out pocket. I grab the flashlight from the ledge. Then, hanging on to my underhanded grip, I walk my feet down the Chimney's walls.

Three feet below me, another boulder forms a safe spot to land. I let go and jump. The beam of the flashlight bobbles, lighting up random bumps and cracks in the rock. The boulder is smooth and round. It rests on the large rock ledge that almost blocks the entire Chimney. Lying on my stomach, I slither down the boulder, sliding and scraping until my feet touch the ledge. I shine the flashlight around, looking for the hole that leads farther down the Chimney. "Rusty?"

"Down here."

I follow his voice to the hole in the rock ledge, where one stretcher pole sticks up through the gap. I crouch and shine my beam down. Jeb's face looks ghastly pale. Below him, Rusty's face peers up at me, strained and worried. The stretcher lies on the diagonal slab that leads up to the hole. Obviously, Rusty was trying to push Jeb up the slab. But one of the stretcher poles got wedged into a corner beneath the rock ledge.

"I see it, Rusty. It's the pole on this side."

Laying the flashlight on the ledge, I reach into the hole and grab the stretcher pole.

My face hovers so close to Jeb's that I can feel his heat, hear his rapid, shallow breaths. He's muttering something about a forty-yard pass.

"Interception!" he mumbles.

"Have you got it, Vanisha?" Rusty calls up.

"It's jammed in really tight. Can you pull from your end?"

We tug and pull. The pole budges a bit, then a little bit more, scraping against the underside of the rock ledge. *This is stupid. It's got to come.* I take a firmer grip, brace my feet and yank hard. The pole jerks free, and I whiplash backward, whacking my head against the rock wall. My knee bangs the flashlight, and it rolls over the edge, its beam disappearing down the gap in the rock.

"Rusty?" I blink in the dimness. The hole in the ledge glows with the light of Rusty's headlamp.

"Vanisha, are you okay?"

"Yeah, I'm okay. Where's the flashlight?"

"Jeb's got it."

"Jeb's got it? Jeb isn't even conscious."

"It's laying on him. Reach down."

I crawl to the edge of the opening. "Jeb. Come on, Jeb. Pass me the flashlight."

It's useless. He can't hear me. Or if he can, he can't make sense of what I'm saying. I lie on my belly and reach down over his sweating-hot chest. I feel a rapid heartbeat but don't know if it's his or mine. At last my fingers hook the flashlight. By its light, I adjust the poles, make sure they're pointing straight up through the gap in the ledge. I check the knots on the rope. Everything's fine now.

"Good work," Rusty says.

"I'll give you the signal when I'm back on belay."

Retracing my steps to the belay station on the ledge, I realize I'm shaking. Even the easy moves require an effort that seems almost too much. How much longer can this night go on? How much strength have I got left? I reach the ledge and start to haul on the rope. Inch by inch, the stretcher rises until at last we haul Jeb onto the ledge.

Rusty squeezes my hand. "We're nearly there, Vanisha."

Nearly, but not quite. "How do you want to do this?" I look up the Chimney. It's eight feet to the top.

"You go first," says Rusty. "Once you get to the top, I'll pull Jeb up with the rope. If you can grab the poles and get his head above ground, I'll push the rest of the stretcher up from the bottom."

I nod. "Sounds good."

I place my back against one wall of the Chimney and my feet against the other. My thighs shake. *Focus. Straighten my legs. Push my back up the wall. Walk my legs up until my knees are bent. Straighten my legs again. Push my back up the wall. Walk my legs up.*

At last I reach the top, grab the slings wrapped around the trees and haul myself over the edge.

I turn to call down to Rusty.

But a hand grabs my arm in an iron-hard grip.

# chapter nineteen

I scream.

The hand yanks me to my feet. Another hand clamps my mouth shut. I can't see the man holding me from behind, but I know he's big, strong. His brawny arms are covered in tattoos. *Blade.*

Part of me knows I can't escape. Yet my instincts tell me to fight. I kick wildly, aiming my blows backward against his shins. I squirm and thrash and dig my fingernails into his arms.

He laughs, his breath hot in my ear, and drags me toward the campsite. I shoot out an arm and grab the closest thing in sight— the skinny trunk of a young tree. I kick my legs and wrap them around it too. His hand slips off my mouth as he tries to rip me off the tree, and I scream again.

Rusty comes out of the Chimney like a cougar leaping from its cave. He jumps on Blade, grabs him by the neck and hauls him backward. The iron-hard hands release me as Blade stumbles back. But he regains his footing and, with a grunt, flips Rusty to the ground.

I spring forward to attack him. He grabs me again, twists my arm behind my back and pulls a gun from his belt. The cold metal barrel presses against my temple.

"One move from you, punk, and your girlfriend's dead."

Rusty looks up. I see helpless anger in his face. Blade lets out a hard nasty laugh. His grip tightens on my arm. I want to scream, but the gun pressed to my head stops me.

"Let her go, Blade," comes a voice from the woods. "Let her go right now, and no one gets hurt."

Loretta steps out of the shadows. She's pointing a hunting rifle straight at Blade's head.

Blade grips me tighter. "What're you doin' here, sweetheart?" he growls.

"Don't 'sweetheart' me," says Loretta. "Let her go."

"You friends with these punks?"

"I just want to get 'em home safe to their mommas," she says. "Now I ain't got time to stand here chitty-chattin'. You let her go, and these kids'll be on their way."

Blade twists my arm harder. "I don't take orders from no waitress," he says.

Loretta cracks a smile. "Oh yes, you do. Because unlike your gun, mine has got bullets in it."

Blade says nothing. I can feel his hesitation.

"I took 'em out while y'all were sleepin'," Loretta says. "You don't think I'm fool enough to hang out in the woods with a bunch of boys who've got loaded guns, now do you?"

"You're bluffing," he growls.

"Wanna bet?"

Suddenly, he shoves the gun barrel harder against my temple. I close my eyes and think of everyone I'd want to say goodbye to: Rusty, Jeb, my mom.

*Click*.

That's all.

An empty click.

The gun falls away from my head.

My breath comes out in a rush, half sob, half laughter.

"I wasn't bluffin' then. And I ain't bluffin' now," says Loretta. "You let her go, or there is going to be one very unfortunate hunting accident in about three seconds. One...two..."

She takes a step forward. The grip on my arm releases. I spring away from Blade and hurry to Rusty. He scrambles to his feet, winded but not hurt.

"You kids get your friend outta that hole and into my truck. I'll keep my eye on Hotshot here," says Loretta.

"What about the others?" I ask.

"Still passed out. I checked. Now y'all git goin' before they wake up."

"Yes, ma'am," says Rusty. "Right away."

It takes a few minutes to hoist Jeb out of the Chimney and carry the stretcher through the woods to Loretta's truck. We lay him in the flatbed with a blanket underneath him and another one thrown on top. Rusty sits in the back with Jeb. Loretta hands him the rifle.

"I can't use this while I'm drivin'," she says. "You keep an eye out behind us."

She climbs into the cab, and I climb in beside her. "I reckon I'm gonna have to find a new job," she says as she puts the truck in gear. "Them biker boys were my best tippers."

It takes her two hours to drive us home to Fayetteville, the nearest city with a hospital. While Rusty sits in the back with Jeb, I call our parents on Loretta's cell phone. I try to tell them what's happening without upsetting them.

My mom's voice is hoarse with sleep and anxiety. "Are you sure you're okay, honey? Are you sure?" she says.

"I'm fine," I say, though I still feel shaky and I'm ready to drop with exhaustion. The hardest call is to Jeb's mom, who starts freaking out. "I need to talk to him! Right now! Put him on the phone!" she yells. The pitch of her voice rises higher and higher.

"He's sleeping right now," I sort of lie. "Meet us at the hospital, okay? We're almost there."

The sun is rising when Loretta finally pulls up in front of the Emergency doors. A couple of paramedics hurry over to unload Jeb onto a proper stretcher. He doesn't seem any better, but he doesn't seem any worse either. He's still sweating and mumbling. As the paramedics wheel the stretcher into the hospital, Jeb's parents rush over, half crazed with worry. A nurse leads them away while the stretcher is whisked into the operating room.

I get choked up when I see my mom. She's wearing a necklace of wooden beads, a long, purple paisley dress and Birkenstocks. It's a look that's embarrassed me all year, here in the land of Southern belles and sorority girls. But suddenly, I don't care. I don't care if she starts quoting poetry in the hospital waiting room and all the nurses and ambulance attendants look at her like she's a complete nutso. All I care about is how glad I am to see her again. Her hug is warm, soft and fierce. Suddenly, I find myself crying on her shoulder.

Loretta calls the state troopers and hands over her video of the deputy and the bikers. We each give statements to the police while the doctors operate on Jeb. They pump him full of antibiotics, remove the bullet and sew up the damage to his insides.

The trooper who interviews me can barely believe I hiked all the way into Mount Judea alone.

"You've got a very brave young woman there," he says to my mom.

"Yes, she is." Mom puts her arm around me. "And I hope she never has to prove it again."

## chapter twenty

I hit the sack later that afternoon and sleep until the next morning. When I come down for breakfast, Mom's in her housecoat sitting on a packing box, making notes on an article she's submitting to a poetry journal.

She stands up to hug me. "Hi, sleepyhead."

I burrow my face into the shoulder of her soft terrycloth housecoat and hug her longer than usual. "Morning, Mom."

She sits down again and scribbles something in the margin of her article. The article's about a writer named John Donne who's been dead since the seventeenth century. Her forehead is crinkled, as though whatever tiny word she's changing is a matter of earth-shattering importance. Better her than me, I think. The familiar knot tightens in my stomach. The knot I've been feeling whenever I think about starting university. This will be me, I realize. Sitting in my housecoat, writing essays about dead poets, studying to be...what? A professor, like my mom?

I love my mom. But I don't want her life.

I glance up to where our kitchen clock used to be. But it's already disappeared into a packing box.

"What time is it?"

"About eleven."

"When do we have to get going?"

"The moving truck's not coming till this evening."

"Do we have anything for breakfast?"

"Sorry, honey. Everything's packed." She fishes in her pocket and hands me some cash. "Why don't you go and get yourself something? And bring me back a coffee."

"Sure."

I throw on some clothes and walk down the street to the coffee shop. The world feels surreal. I can hardly believe I'm back in Fayetteville, surrounded by cars and stores and houses, when less than twenty-four hours ago, I was fighting for survival in a cave in the woods.

You'd think that, after all that happened last night, I'd never want to set foot in the woods again. But in fact, the opposite is true. In town, I feel strange and disconnected. Last night in the woods, I felt focused. I knew my purpose.

I had a task to do, and I did it. I pulled Edge of Flight. I hiked into town alone. I helped rescue Jeb from the cave. I'm not saying I saved him single-handedly. Far from it. But that's not the point. I don't want to be a lone hero. What I want is to be part of a team that accomplishes something worthwhile. Like the team that saved Jeb's life.

I think about what Rusty said when I stood at the base of Edge of Flight, doubting if I could pull the crux. *Commit, Vanisha. You can do it. You've just got to commit.*

By the time I get home from the coffee shop, I know what I have to do.

Almost all of our household stuff is in boxes, but Mom's computer still hasn't been packed up.

"Can I use your computer for a bit?" I ask as I hand her the coffee.

"I'll need it in about an hour."

"That's okay. I just have to print off a couple of things."

It takes me far less than an hour to print off the forms I need and write a short letter. I dig out some documents from one of the boxes in my room—birth certificate, high school diploma, my final report card. I throw it all into a bag and head to the climbing gym where Rusty works.

At 1:00 PM on a weekday, the gym's pretty much empty. It smells, as always, of chalk dust and sweaty feet. One bare-chested wall rat is practicing his moves in the bouldering section. Over in the beginners' section, a couple of novices are learning the ropes. The gym owner, a hard-core climber in his thirties, is halfway up an overhang, setting a new route in the toughest section of the gym. Rusty sits in a tattered office-surplus chair behind the plywood counter that serves as the gym's front desk. He's hanging up the phone when I walk in. He looks dead-tired. Not a look you usually see on Rusty.

"That was Jeb's dad," he says.

"How's Jeb doing?"

"The guy's a horse."

"Meaning?"

"He opened his eyes this morning and asked the doc if he could make football tryouts next week."

"No way."

"Yeah, way." Rusty grins. "Doc told him to stick to the sidelines for now."

"So is he better?"

"Getting better. No visitors except family for now. But they're saying the operation was smooth. Too early to tell about organ damage. They've got to run a bunch of tests."

I nod. "He'll pull through."

"Yeah," Rusty says.

"I wish I could see him before I leave."

"When's that, Vanisha?"

"I don't know. Sometime this evening. It depends when the moving van shows up." I pull the papers out of my bag and come around to Rusty's side of the counter. "I need you to help me with something before I go."

Rusty looks at the papers. Then he looks back at me. "Johnson State College. Search-and-Rescue Technician?"

"Yeah. It's a new program. I'm applying to get in. I can't make the fall semester, obviously. But I might be able to start after Christmas."

"That's awesome, Vanisha."

"Yeah. I think it's the right thing."

"What about the University of Vermont? Your BA?"

I pull a copy of the email I sent earlier and show it to him. It's short and to the point.

*To Whom it May Concern,*
*I am writing to withdraw from the BA program at the University of Vermont. Due to a change of plans, I will not be enrolling in the program this fall. Please refund my tuition deposit.*
*Sincerely,*
*Vanisha Lindhurst*

Rusty hands it back. "That about says it all," he says.

"Yeah." I shove the paper back into my bag. It makes me nervous to read it. It's such a big decision. If I think about it too much, I'm afraid I'll second-guess myself and back out. I haven't told Mom what I'm doing yet. I'm sure she'd try to talk me out of it.

I turn back to the application forms. "I need you to help me with this. I have to write a three-hundred-word essay on why I want to get into the program. So what am I supposed to say?"

Rusty shrugs. "Just say you met these two really cool climbing dudes in Arkansas and it changed your life."

"Come on, Rusty. Seriously."

"Okay." He opens up a word-processing program on the gym's computer. "Why don't you start by talking about how we rescued Jeb?"

It takes us a couple of hours to finish the essay, with a few interruptions from people signing in and out of the gym. I fill out the rest of the forms and make photocopies of the other documents I need to submit.

Finally, Rusty goes on a break and we walk to the post office. "So what's your mom going to say about this?" he asks.

"I've been thinking about that. She'll probably give me a big lecture, tell me I'm making a huge mistake. And maybe she'll refuse to pay my tuition." I shrug. "I've got a little money saved. I'll get a job if I have to. Maybe a student loan. I don't think she'll kick me out or anything."

"You need to strike her with her own weapon," says Rusty.

147

"What do you mean?"

"You know, find some really awesome line of poetry that explains exactly what you're doing."

I think about that as the clerk figures out how much postage I need for express mail.

"How about this: *Two roads diverged in a wood, and I– / I took the one less traveled by, / And that has made all the difference.*"

"That's good," says Rusty. "Yeah, that rocks. What is it?"

"Robert Frost. 'The Road Not Taken.'"

"That's what it's all about," says Rusty. "You've got to take one road or the other. You've got to decide. And no one else can decide for you. It's your decision. Because it's your road. You're the one who has to walk it. Not your mom. Not anyone else."

"Yeah, that's right," I say.

"So hit her with it. See what she has to say to that."

I pay for the postage, and the clerk pops the letter in the big mailbag behind the counter.

"You know," I say to Rusty, "that's not a bad idea."

"Thanks. I'm not just a dumb jock, you know."

"I never said you were."

We walk side by side out of the post office and onto Fayetteville's Main Street. It's got that quaint small-town atmosphere, cafés, gift shops, a sizzling-bacon smell from the Ozark Mountain Smokehouse.

"I gotta get back to work," Rusty says.

"Yeah. I should get home in case the moving van shows up."

Neither of us moves though. Then suddenly we are touching hands. Suddenly, we're holding each other. My cheek is pressed against his chest. My arms are wrapped around his warm, strong back.

"Y'all come back and see us now sometime, y'hear?" Rusty says, doing his best imitation of a Southern momma.

I wipe a tear away on his T-shirt. "Don't make me cry, Rusty."

He strokes my hair. "Don't cry, Vanisha."

But I am crying. It's strange how I spent my whole year feeling I didn't fit in. And now I realize there are things I'll miss about this place. I'll miss the beauty of the Ozark Mountains, the p'kaahn pie, Loretta and her Southern charm.

I'll miss Jeb, even though he's a big goof. And I'll miss Rusty. I'll really miss Rusty.

We pull apart from each other at last. The sun casts long shadows down the street. We promise to keep in touch. But you can't touch someone when you're a thousand miles away. Rusty turns and walks back toward the climbing gym. His legs swing with an easy, confident stride. It's a stride that says he'll master any route he encounters. There's a little of that swing in my stride, too, as I turn and walk toward home. Though we're each going our separate ways, I know I'm going toward my future.

The future I've chosen for myself.

# Glossary

**Anchor**—a fixed object used to secure a rope used for climbing or rappelling

**Arête**—a sharp outward-facing corner on a steep rock face

**Belay**—to protect a roped climber from falling by passing the rope through or around any type of friction-enhancing belay device

**Belay device**—a mechanical device used to create friction when belaying by putting bends in the rope

**Bombproof**—slang for totally secure; usually refers to an anchor

**Camming device**—a piece of protective equipment consisting of toothed gears that can be retracted by means of a spring-loaded trigger

**Carabiner** (pronounced kar-uh-BEE-ner)—a metal oval or D-shaped ring with a spring catch on one side used for fastening climbing ropes; most often called a "'biner" in climbing slang

**Chimney**–(1) a narrow vertical opening in a rock face; (2) to climb or descend using opposed limb or body pressure against two facing walls

**Climbing harness**–a sewn nylon-webbing device worn around the waist and thighs that is designed to allow a person to safely hang suspended in the air when attached to a rope

**Clipping in**–the process of attaching the rope to an anchor by means of one or more carabiners

**Crux**–the most difficult portion of a climb

**Foothold**–a rock formation that a climber can stand on with one or both feet

**Free-climbing**–climbing without a rope

**Gear-head**–a person who loves acquiring the latest and greatest in climbing gear

**GRIGRI**–a belay device that is self-locking under load; invented and manufactured by Petzl

**Handhold**–a rock formation that can be gripped by a climber's hand

**Hex (hexcentric)**–six-sided nut of varying size that is placed or wedged in cracks for passive protection for a lead climber; the nut has holes that are threaded with cord or cable wire to allow a carabiner to be clipped into it

**Jug**—a large, easily held handhold

**Layback**—a climbing move that involves pulling on the hands while pushing on the feet

**Lead**—to be the lead climber on a route

**Lead climber**—the first climber to ascend the route and secure the rope to the cliff

**Microhold**—a tiny handhold

**Nut**—a metal wedge attached to a wire loop that is inserted into cracks for protection

**Off-route**—an object (often a tree or a man-made object) that the climber is not supposed to use as a hold if the route is to be accomplished to technical perfection

**On-route**—an object (often a tree) that is acceptable as a handhold on a route

**Pistol-hold grip**—a handhold in the shape of a pistol

**Rappel**—to descend a cliff or wall by rope, using friction to control speed

**Rope in**—to tie the rope to one's harness, in preparation for climbing

**Pro**—protective gear such as cams, nuts and hexes

**Top rope**—to climb a route using an anchor point that is set at the top of the climb

**Top-out**—to complete a route by ascending over the top of the structure being climbed

**Wedge**—another word for a nut

## Acknowledgments

I would like to thank my husband Mark for supporting my writing career, and my editor Christi Howes for pummeling my manuscript into shape. Also, thanks to all of my climbing buddies over the years, especially to the real Chris, Michael and Rusty, who took me climbing in Arkansas' Ozark Mountains.

Kate Jaimet is an Ottawa author and journalist who recently began a freelance career after many years as a daily newspaper reporter for the *Ottawa Citizen*. Her first book in the Orca Sports series, *Slam Dunk*, was chosen as a Junior Library Guild selection and was included in the Canadian Children's Book Centre's Best Books for Kids & Teens. Kate learned to rock climb in Germany and now has a bouldering wall in her basement. For more information, visit www.katejaimet.com.